THE *I AM MARGARET* SERIES

LIBERATION was nominated for the *Carnegie Medal Award 2016* and won 3rd place for 'Teen & Young Adult Fiction' in the *Catholic Press Association 2016 Book Awards*.

I AM MARGARET, THE THREE MOST WANTED, LIBERATION, BANE'S EYES & MARGO'S DIARY have been awarded the 'Seal of Approval' by the *Catholic Writers Guild* and *I AM MARGARET* was one of 2 runners-up for the 'Teen & Children's Fiction' *CALA Award 2016*.

PRAISE FOR *I AM MARGARET*

Great style—very good characters and pace.
Definitely a book worth reading, like The Hunger Games.
EOIN COLFER, author of the *Artemis Fowl* books

An intelligent, well-written and enjoyable debut from
a young writer with a bright future.
STEWART ROSS, author of *The Soterion Mission*

One of the best Christian fiction books I have read.
CAT CAIRD, blogger, 'Sunshine Lenses'

PRAISE FOR *SOMEDAY*

"SOMEDAY is an important novella that highlights the largely unsung heroism of persecuted Christians, and should make those of us in 'safe' countries consider: are we ready to count the cost?"
REGINA DOMAN, author of *The Fairytale Novels* and *The Angel In The Waters*

PRAISE FOR *DRIVE!*

"A cross between Jurassic World and Mad Max! I read it 2 times
in 2 da
STEVEN R. MCE

The I AM MARGARET Series:
For Older Teens & Adults

I Am Margaret
The Three Most Wanted
Liberation
Bane's Eyes
Margo's Diary *(Companion Volume)*
Brothers *(A Short Prequel Novella)*

Coming Soon:
The Siege of Reginald Hill (*A Sequel Novella*)

The YESTERDAY & TOMORROW Series:
For Older Teens & Adults

Someday: A Novella

Coming soon:
Tomorrow's Dead

The UNSPARKED Series
For Teens & Adults

1:0 – DRIVE!

Coming Soon:
1.1 – A Truly Raptor-ous Welcome

Standalone Works:
For Teens & Adults

Elfling

Coming soon:
Mandy Lamb & The Full Moon

MARGO'S (attempted) DIARY
& NOTEBOOK

CORINNA TURNER

Look, here's that name again. They really wanted to be sure you'd know who made the notebook, didn't they?

Bane, just stop scribbling everywhere!

So I'm not allowed to say that I like this little doodle thingie?

No, you're not!

unSeen

CONTENTS

Plus a lot of graffiti
from me!
Graffiti is the word, Bane!
You're a menace!

It almost feels like I could just call this diary:
'Visitors'!

27th October (20 today)
U gave me this nice notebook today for my birthday, so I think I'm going to try to keep a diary! I'm sure I'll have loads to write about Lucas Mark when he arrives!

19th December (20)
What a very Margo-centric way of marking the date!
Oh shut up, Bane!
Bane's Birthday! We had a lovely romantic dinner together, enjoy some uninterrupted time together while we can! Not long now. Little Luc is due in January.
I just find it easier to keep track!

30th December (20)
This diary is not going very well!
(It's really not, is it?)
Bane!

12th January (20)
Luc born today! More or less bang on time! What a good baby! The less said about the 'arriving' the better; now he's out, I don't care! Pope Cornelius is going to be his Godfather. What a lucky baby he is. Anyway, I'm putting this down because I want to cuddle our baby again. Sorry diary, you cannot compete.
Thought I was going to pass out. So glad to be a guy, today!
Er- YOU'RE complaining? Seriously, Bane?
I'll have you know, it was highly traumatic. :)
Actually, I thought you were amazing. xxx
xxx

4th March (20)
Unicorn told me some interesting things today. So did Fox. I must write them in here some time. Haven't got time

1

now. All about how Snakey got his nickname. It's not what I thought!

Are you sure about that, Margo? Asking seriously...

8ᵗʰ March

Okay, so I was thinking about it, and perhaps I'd better not write about that in here. The stuff about U was top secret, and Snakey didn't like people knowing about what happened, so it feels wrong to write it all down, even if it is a <u>private</u> diary. It's not the sort of thing I'm likely to forget. *Look up this word, Bane!!!*

Means: do not read - unless it's left open on my chair, desk or pillow!

14th May (20)

Okay, so something happened today that I really wanted to record. But it was obviously going to be a really long entry and I couldn't face handwriting it, so it's the old print, cut and paste. Because I was typing this, it's ended up sounding pretty much like one of my books, actually, but that's okay, it just means I've put more detail down. *More fun to read, too!*

Anyway, I was walking along the side aisle of St Peter's when I noticed the man balancing a proCamera on his twisted, claw-like left hand while he took a shot of the main basilica. I stopped dead—looked more closely... and it *was*... *Dum, Dum, Dah! Bane, stop it!*

When I waved a hand behind my back, a guy who'd been drifting along behind, apparently admiring the paintings, and another who'd knelt to pray at a side altar as soon as I stopped both seemed to lose interest in what they were doing and headed towards me. I hastily made another gesture, the one that meant, 'I think it's fine, just pay attention,' and their interest in art and prayer returned to them. *Does Eduardo know they were SO obvious? Bane,*

I went a few steps closer to the man with the camera. "Watkins...?" *just STOP, or I'm going to get white-out from the store.*

The camera slipped from his hand, landing safely on the end of the carry strap around his neck, and he spun around. "Margaret?" He sounded astonished.

I couldn't help laughing. "You must know I live here, surely?"

"Well, of course, but... it didn't occur to me I'd run into you."

I'd not thought about it before I approached him, but suddenly I felt awkward. After all, the last time I'd seen him I'd shot him with a nonLee, stripped him to his underwear and left him to face the music. *Hahahaha!*

He didn't seem to share my awkwardness. "How are you, lass? And your wee lad? And your bigger lad, come to that."

"We're all very well. Bane's looking after Luc, I was just having a break. Uh... how are you?"

He was out of a job partly because of me, as well...

He seemed to follow my train of thought this time. "I ended up retiring slightly early – along with everyone else. And very happy I was about it, I assure you."

"The retiring, or the everyone else retiring?" I couldn't help asking.

"Both," he said cheerfully. "You've done a helluva good thing, Margaret Verrall."

"Me and the voting population of the EuroBloc," I pointed out quickly.

"Including me," he grinned.

I grinned back, delighted. Even EGD Security had voted against Sorting! Some of them, anyway... "Er, how's Sally?" Watkins' equally nice, female, colleague...

He pulled a slight face. "Well, she's living with her brother's widow. She takes care of the kids so her sister-in-law can work longer hours. The boys don't really see enough of their mum, but Sally tried for ages to get a job with no luck. Sally's got a bit of pension, and so has David's widow, and so they're comfortable. Sally voted no, too, you know, and she's not sorry, but she gets a bit down, thinking she'll never work again. But I reckon she will. Thanks to you. I'm glad of an opportunity to thank you for those posts you put up about giving people like us second chances."

I shrugged, blushing. "So I pointed out that they'd all been paying your wages for decades. It's the truth."

"Sometimes it helps if people hear it." A less pleasant smile curled his lips. "Did you hear about Finchley?"

"The bit about having to go into protective custody to escape a mob or the bit where he confessed to goodness knows what in order to stay locked up?"

"I think most of it was true, you know."

I shrugged. Finchley's confession had covered everything from drugs possession to the one charge I knew was true. "It *was* you who told Lucas what he did, wasn't it?"

Watkins shrugged. "That woman was a fool to let something like that go. He'd only have tried again."

"Yeah, I bet he would." Only he'd probably have chosen someone like Sarah the next time... I swallowed bile and tried to push down the fury that still surged up inside at the thought of Finchley. *Forgiveness. Forgiveness.*

"So, uh, what are you doing here?" I asked.

"Oh, well, I have that hearty pension of mine so I'd no need to go begging for another job. I thought I'd go round the bloc, see the sites while I've still got a bit of use of the old hand." He displayed it to me matter-of-factly. It looked like he could hardly straighten his fingers now. "Couldn't miss St Peter's, could I? And..." he hesitated. "Well, to be honest, I was quite curious to see where the old man ended up. Who'd have thought it would be here?"

It took me a moment to realize he was using 'old man' as slang for a respected superior... that he was talking about Lucas, easily twenty years his junior.

"He was very happy here," I said, swallowing a lump in my throat. *No tearing up, Margo, it's been almost a year...* "Uh, would you like to... pay your respects?"

Watkins looked startled. "You mean... visit the grave?"

"Umhmm."

"Would I be allowed?"

I had to smile. "If you're with me. I live here, you know."

"Well... yes. I would."

"Come on, then. Though... you may get a black mark for entering the Vatican Free State."

"Only a little one, seeing that I'll be leaving again."

I led the way down the side aisle, and the VSS agents drifted casually after me again, sticking a bit closer than usual. I didn't really think Watkins was going to try and hurt me, but I'd got in the habit of being particularly careful whilst Luc was inside me.

We went through the doorway that provided the main access from the basilica to the rest of the state and stopped in front of the security desk.

"Hi Snail, can I get a visitor's pass for Mr. Watkins, please?" It was only as I said it, that I realized I didn't actually know Watkins' first name.

"Of course." I'd spoken in Latin automatically, and Snail replied in the same, then switched to Esperanto. "Could I see your ID card, please, Mr. Watkins?"

Watkins handed it over and Snail made a show of checking the image and information before casually putting it down on the desk—or rather, onto a concealed flat card reader. He began filling something in on the computer screen, sneaking a look at Watkins' ID database entry while he was at it. Almost at once a hint of a frown crossed his face. He hit a couple more keys—pinging Eduardo, no doubt—and smiled politely at Watkins. "Length of planned visit?"

Watkins looked at me.

"A day pass will be fine. That's anything less than staying overnight," I explained to Watkins.

Snail took his time filling in the simple form, and was running out of ways to stall when, surprise, surprise, Eduardo came prowling up. He began to root around in the desk drawer as though he'd simply come to get something—he tried very hard not to advertise to the EuroGov that he could access their system—but he did glance at me and at Watkins. "Friend of yours, Margaret?"

"Er... well, yes, basically," I said, and gave my eyebrows a slight waggle—*yes, Eduardo, I do know he's ex-EGD Security.* Snail was only doing his job.

Eduardo accepted my non-verbal communication and turned to Snail. "Have you seen the lists?"

"Jack took them earlier," said Snail.

5

"Right." Eduardo gave me a polite nod and headed off again.

Snail handed Watkins a visitor's pass and locked the ID card in a little box on the wall. "We do a swap when you come out," he informed Watkins.

Watkins clipped the pass to his collar happily enough. Snail glanced at his camera. "Oh, I must inform you that your photos will need to be reviewed before you leave. Alternatively, you can leave the camera here."

Watkins put a hand to the camera rather protectively. "I'll hang onto it. I won't point it at anything security-related."

"Well, as long as you understand we'll have to check."

"Oh, I understand about security concerns." With a smile and a nod to Snail, he followed me past the desk.

As we headed along the stone corridors, Watkins was too busy staring around to talk, beyond an occasional mutter of, "No one is ever going to believe where I am right now!"

"Take a picture," I suggested, amused.

"I don't want my memory card wiping."

"They wouldn't do that. They'd just delete individual photos."

"Well... Will you tell me if you think I'm pointing it anywhere I shouldn't?"

"Of course."

Watkins was soon snapping away happily. "There's so much history here," he enthused, photographing a pair of motionless Swiss guards. "I thought about coming when the EuroBloc had it, you know—they were showing behind the scenes, for a price—but I didn't really want to encourage them, it being bare-faced theft, and everything. But this is fantastic. Much nicer to see it occupied in time-honored fashion. Huh, there's a real nun..." He pointed the camera eagerly.

"A religious sister, actually," I remarked. "But I won't bamboozle you with the distinction. But you can photograph sisters at home, now, surely?"

"Well... in theory. I've only seen one, since the permanent lifting of the Suppression. And I didn't have my camera with me."

Watkins went on clicking away as we came out of the network of buildings and headed for the gardens cum graveyard. The sun was shining and it was a lovely day. Perhaps Bane and I could take a walk later, give Luc some fresh air.

But Watkins' photography became more hesitant as we got in among the flower beds and gravestones. "This is a bit weird," he said after a moment or two. "It looks just like some grand old formal garden... until you look closely."

I shrugged. "There's not a lot of space to waste, in here. Anyway, we don't think of graves as scary, the way nonBelievers do. They're only sleeping."

Watkins merely grunted in response to that. I couldn't say why, exactly, but I'd always had him pegged as an atheist. The kind who would probably call himself a humanist. But we'd hardly been able to discuss such things in the Facility.

"Well, here we are." I turned into a secluded dell and stopped by one of the pair of graves there. The purple fuchsia was flourishing, almost tripled in size since I'd planted it the previous summer. The white one on the other grave was equally spectacular. I brushed the gravestones with my fingers, murmuring my customary, 'Hello, Lucas; hello, Father Mark' under my breath so as not to freak Watkins out.

Watkins was standing rather awkwardly by the grave, looking a little bemused as he read the headstone. It just said:

Lucas James Everington

Sinner

✝

And the years he'd lived.

"That's a bit... brief," said Watkins. 'Harsh' was probably the word he'd swallowed. "I thought you lot had forgiven him."

I looked at the stark words and sighed. "We did and we have. He still didn't entirely like himself, though. He told me that's all he wanted, just the day after his baptism – I can't even remember how it came up. When only a few days later, he... Well, I felt I should honor his wishes."

'And only the years, for pity's sake,' he'd said. 'No one is ever going to care whether I was born in March, April or May, let alone what day. I don't care myself.'

Had he been laying his plan even then, knowing how it might turn out?

"Did you want to say anything?" I asked Watkins, to distract myself from the bad memories.

"There's nothing left but moldering bones, lass." But after a long, long silence, he spoke anyway, very softly. "Well, sir, I couldn't have imagined when you arrived that you'd end up in the ground before me. Such a nice young man. I don't suppose I'll ever know what happened that changed you so much, but I'm glad you found a home here, even if it wasn't for long."

He gave a firm nod, and it was clear he'd said what he wanted to say. His words sparked a storm of curiosity in me, though. He'd known Lucas for so long.

"Is this his fuchsia?" Watkins asked. "I think you mentioned it on your blog."

"Yes, this purple one grew from his seeds. They were in the parcel you sent for him."

Watkins' head swiveled to look at me. "That was for *you?* But why? The charges against him were false... What else was in it?"

I hesitated. The vote was won, and we'd kept the pressure turned well up on the EuroGov so far to combat any attempt at regression on their part. But. If the EGD ever managed to reopen the Facilities, they might revise their security procedures – but they might not.

"The charges were certainly false," I said guardedly. "But he did do one thing to help our cause—but only after the escape. When he was sure he was doomed."

Watkins sighed. "Yes, I sensed that. I felt so bad for him I didn't ask as many questions as I might have done. You're not going to tell me either, are you?"

"Sorry. It's still rather valuable information."

"Information..." I meant the identity of what had been sent, but Watkins' hands rose, tracing the shape of the remembered parcel in the air, a look of sudden intentness on his face. "He *did* burn all his documents. That was the only charge that was true. All the Facility paperwork, records, the lot. I thought he was just getting his own back—though it seemed foolish to give them hard evidence for so little gain, and he was not a foolish man. But *that* wasn't the revenge, was it... He sent you his security manual. That's why you were able to go through all those Facilities like a knife through butter. You had every scrap of information, the works. He sent it. Chairman's innards, *I* sent it to you. If they'd found it..."

He looked a bit green at the mere thought. "Well," he went on, after a moment of silence. "I'm not sorry you ended up with it, but I'm none too sure I'd have dared do it if he'd told me. Though I remember what he said when he gave it to me. He said, 'If anyone asks, I ordered you.' So I did know there could be trouble. I just didn't realize I was... bringing down the EGD!"

"They're not totally brought down yet," I said. "Still all sorts of awful breeding regulations in place. Uh... you won't mention your... speculations... to anyone else, will you?"

Watkins snorted. "Are you mad? I've no wish to share the Major's fate. I'll take it to my grave, lass, never fear."

He seemed to mean it, thank goodness. But perhaps it would be kindest not to mention this to Eduardo. At least, not unless we actually needed to use the manual again...

The first clock began to strike the hour and I checked my watch. Two o'clock. I needed to get home. Luc would be getting hungry and the food would be done.

"I suppose I'd better be going," said Watkins.

"Would you like to stay for lunch? Bane should have taken it out of the oven by now, it's all ready."

Pleasure warred with uncertainty on Watkins' face. "Well... if you'd really like to have me."

It was strange to be around Watkins again, here, on my own turf, as it were. It brought the Facility back to me, yet... whenever the dorm door had opened, and Watkins' face had appeared, we'd all felt safe. He wasn't unwelcome. "This way, then."

There was a slight delay at the entrance to my apartment block, while the guard on duty got clearance for Watkins to enter, but soon enough I was unlocking the door I still had to keep locked, Eduardo's orders.

Bane was lying on the floor, apparently demonstrating to Luc just how easy crawling was really. Luc was lying on his tummy, gurgling with laughter. I watched, amused, until Bane noticed I had a guest with me and scrambled hastily to his feet, scooping our darling little boy up and settling him carefully in his arms. "Another guest, Margo?"

Another... ah. Hadn't thought of that. Oh well. "This is Watkins, Bane." I took a quick peep at the visitor's pass. "William Watkins."

"Huh." Bane stepped forward, freeing one hand from his precious burden and offering it. "Margo had a guard in the Facility called Watkins..." He trailed off as his eyes fell on the twisted fingers of Watkins' left hand. "Aww..." he glanced at Luc and substituted what he'd been going to say for a plaintive, "Margo!" his hand retreating...

"Shake, Bane," I said sternly. "Watkins is staying for lunch."

Bane sighed, shook, then suddenly froze, an expression of horror creeping onto his face. "Lunch..." he muttered.

I sniffed, suddenly noticing the slight burnt smell in the air. "Bane! How is it you can time a mission down to the millisecond but you can't pull food out of the oven after half an hour!" I stormed into the kitchen to inspect the damage. *Fair point, Margo. I really will try to do better!*

"I'm sorry, Margo," Bane followed me penitently. "I got distracted. I'm *sure* Luc was trying to crawl..."

"He's only just started holding his head up, Bane." But I was somewhat mollified, all the same. I also found our son very distracting.

Pulling a pan out of the oven, I took the lid off. The shepherd's pie was blackened around the edges, but... "Well, you're lucky, Bane, I think most of the central part will be fine. Good job I made a big one."

Luc began to whimper, either wanting my attention, or hungry, perhaps both. I took him from Bane and carried him back to where Watkins stood, pretending, in proper British fashion, not to have noticed the minor culinary crisis.

"Watkins, this is Luc. Lucas Mark Verrall. Luc, this nice gentleman is Watkins. He helped look after your mummy for a while, once."

"That's a generous way of putting it," sighed Watkins, looking at Luc, who stopped fretting for a moment to peer back. "Lovely little lad."

"Well, I think so," I agreed, as Luc began threatening to cry again.

"Margo, you feed Luc, I'll finish off the meal," said Bane, still in apologetic mode.

I gestured Watkins to the sofa and settled myself in the armchair with Luc, unbuttoning my dress, at which Watkins looked greatly alarmed. But the dress's cape-thingy saved him from any serious embarrassment.

"Oh, I should mention," I said, once Luc was sucking happily, "we've a couple of other people coming to lunch. I didn't think about it before, but..."

A knock at the door cut me off. Bane went to get it. "Hi, U; Hi, Jane."

About a month ago we—or at any rate, I—had been stunned when fellow former Salperton reAssignee Jane had showed up with Eduardo's latest bunch of VSS recruits. She was a pretty committed Believer now, wonder of wonders—though some cynical part of me couldn't help wondering if it didn't have a lot to do with it being the way of life most detested by the EuroGov—and policing a small, peaceful Free Town in Africa for the rest of her life did not appeal to her. She wanted to fight for the cause, she wanted to be where the action was and she wanted it badly enough to have passed VSS selection.

The laypeople in the State were fairly equally balanced when it came to the sexes, and the priests and sisters balanced each other out pretty well, but the various guard units were heavily skewed to men. Mostly young men. Especially with the vote won, the arrival of any pretty young woman caused tremendous interest in these quarters, especially among those actually senior enough to marry. Most of our guard friends had been finding excuses to drop around and casually pump me for information concerning how Jane felt about them.

Jane was no better. Committed to her new faith she might now be, but she clearly didn't plan on remaining celibate longer than it took to find the right marriage partner.

Right now she was with Unicorn, though, the chastest and most confirmed bachelor in the state, so they'd probably both come from being on duty. U had actually kind of invited himself to dinner today, or as close as his exquisite manners would allow, but he was always welcome.

"Hi, Margo," Jane came straight over, unfastening her glossy mane of black hair and tossing it back. "How's the cutie pie..." She saw Watkins and started. "*Holy*..." she finished it off with something that made U wince and me frown. Luc wasn't talking yet, and I certainly didn't want *that* to be his first word.

Her colleague's wince had more effect than my frown. Jane's coffee and cream cheeks darkened slightly. "Uh, sorry. Watkins, what the h... um, what on earth are you doing here?"

Watkins had gone very red too, clearly not so sure of his welcome with Jane. "Uh... Well, I ran into Margaret whilst sightseeing in St Peters, and she invited me to lunch."

"Oh." Jane frowned for another moment, as though surprised it could be explained so simply, then seemed to conclude that yes, it really could. U had come over to stand beside her, so she said, "Well, anyway, hello Watkins. Never thought I'd see you again. This is Jack. Jack, this is Watkins. He used to help keep us locked in the Facility."

U's head rose slightly, his eyes narrowing.

"He used to keep the Finchleys in line, as well," I said quietly.

Jane pulled a face. "Well, that too."

Another knock at the door. Bane let Jon in and dived back into the kitchen.

"You'll never guess who Margo invited to lunch," said Jane, before I could say anything.

"Who?" asked Jon, rather self-consciously smoothing down his black clerical attire. He'd only been in the seminary for a month.

Jane jerked her head meaningfully at Watkins, who spoke rather uncertainly. "Uh, hello Jonathan."

Jon started to frown in puzzlement, then a look of astonishment covered his face. "Watkins." It wasn't a question.

"Yes. I hope you don't mind. Margaret very kindly invited me to lunch."

Jon was already dismissing his surprise. "Fine by me. The more the merrier. How are you?"

Watkins began to repeat what he'd already told me, so I yielded Luc to U, who was hovering hopefully, and went to see what Bane was doing to the food.

Soon enough we were all settled at the table and our Vatican guests were looking expectantly from me to Bane, whilst Watkins reached for a serving spoon, then looked uncertain and drew his hand back when he noticed no one else had moved.

It was Bane's turn, and he didn't go in for long graces, so Watkins wouldn't have to wait long.

"Dear Lord," said Bane, clasping his hands in that rather earnest way I found so endearing. "Thank you for food, family, friends, eyes... and... and for kindness and care even in the darkest of places. Amen."

My heart leapt in delight, whilst Watkins looked so taken aback I thought he might have to wipe his eyes. Bane was trying, and he'd clearly remembered that all I'd ever said about Watkins had been positive. Well, except for my grumbling about his sharp wits, which had nearly scuppered our escape before I'd got the drop on him...

"So I'm telling poor Sally, 'It's all right, Margaret's a nice girl, isn't she?' and all the time my heart's pounding like billy-ho and I'm thinking, 'I hope to goodness these girls *are* as nice as they've always seemed or we're dead as doornails!'"

Now that our plates were empty, Watkins had been talked into telling his side of the escape. "But Margaret waited until Sally wasn't looking to put her out with the nonLee, which made me feel a bit better, then the moment I was busy laying Sally down on the floor, she plugged me too. I woke up with a splitting headache, a distinct lack of clothing, and a specialCorps medic slapping my face. SpecialCorps crawling all over the Facility, in fact; I knew at once you'd all got away.

"Major Everington was prowling around driving them mad with his sardonic replies to their stupid questions and looking—to me, anyway—like he'd have been whistling jauntily if it weren't for the fact he knew he was going to get it in the neck. He caught me in an empty corridor that evening, when the bigwigs had all gone, and gave me the parcel. And the next morning they came for him. Bloody bastards." Watkins paused to drink from his wine glass. "The only person to blame was Wallis," he said bitterly. "And what did they do? Promote her. Pah." He sipped more wine, shaking his head in disgust.

Jon and Jane were shaking their heads as well, and so was I. Captain Gladys Wallis, the girls' warden, had been cruel and abusive. There'd been nothing in the news, but hopefully whatever she was doing now, she'd no power over anyone.

Bane went and made coffees for us all, and we moved to the sofas, U taking the place beside Jane on the two-seater, leaving Bane and me on the three-seater with Watkins. Jon stole Luc and sat on the floor with him in his lap, which solved the problem of another seat. As Watkins began to tell me more about Sally's so far depressingly futile job hunt, Jon was clearly too wrapped up with Luc to listen very closely.

"Uh, Jane," U was saying in a low voice, "I, um, wanted a word, actually..."

"Well, go on, then, it's just us," said Jane. Well, on that sofa, anyway...

U shot Watkins a look, then took a deep breath, as though dismissing the unexpected guest, and focused his vivid blue eyes on Jane again. "Well... I was actually wondering if there was any chance you might like to... that you might consider... taking a turn around the Vatican wall with me?" he finished very fast.

Jane had been here long enough to know she was being asked out. I lost track of what I was saying in reply to Watkins, my ears straining, attention completely grabbed by the other conversation. Jon had fallen silent, mid-coo, and Luc gurgled an objection. Bane's head swiveled sharply towards U, then abruptly back again as he tried to pretend it hadn't. I fought not to allow my own head to turn, not to stare, but out of the corner of my eye I could see the deep crimson that was creeping up U's tense face as the silence lengthened.

Jane was clearly taken aback. U had been one of the first guys she'd grilled me about, but of course I'd had to break it to her that...

"I thought you didn't like girls," she retorted, blunt as ever.

U's face went entirely brick red, but he kept his cool. "I like *you*," he said simply.

Jane's turn to blush, the warm brown of her cheeks darkening. "Well," she... stuttered. "In that case, I'd love to. I mean..." She began to recover herself. "Why not. Yeah, why not. Let's."

Well, that was a first. *Another* first. Jane had turned everyone down so far, on the grounds they hadn't got to know her so must be going entirely on looks. I'd been expecting those with a more serious interest to start making a move soon, so I wasn't surprised that *someone* had seized on the comparative privacy of a Sunday lunch, but... *U?* I was gobsmacked. In a really happy way!

Jane and U. My mind was boggling. The silence in the room was far too obvious. I struggled to remember what I'd been saying...

"Great," U was saying, looking equal parts thrilled and terrified. "That's smashing. What about... tomorrow night? We... don't actually have to walk around the wall, you know, that's just how one asks..."

"Yeah, yeah, Vatican slang, I know," said Jane, but she was smiling, and looked very pleased with herself, in a startled sort of way.

What had I been *saying* to Watkins? *Think, Margo! Or say something else, come on, come on...*

Jon managed to mumble something that made very little sense to Luc, but my mind was still blank.

Watkins, sensing the awkward moment, and no doubt having garnered some notion of the cause, rescued the situation. "Glad I was able to retire, myself," he said heartily, as though there'd been no pause in the conversation.

"Yes, very good," I said stupidly. "I mean... That must have been much nicer for you."

"Than looking for a job. Much nicer," added Bane, sounding just as stupid as me. But this was such a shock. U had seemed as irrecoverably fixed on celibate bachelor-hood as anyone could be. And even if he hadn't been... U and Jane? It just wasn't a combination I'd have thought of.

Jane was so loud and rebellious and, well, prickly. U was the perfect gentleman, so honorable: kind and polite and conscientious. But they were also both keenly intelligent, brave... Jane seemed to be taking to VSS duties like a fish to water... And honorable wasn't the word most people used when describing how Agent Jack Willmott had won the Battle for the Vatican over a pile of un-conscious—and in some cases lifeless—civilians. Clever, cunning, and ruthless, were words more commonly used. Perhaps they had more in common than it seemed on the surface. Perhaps...

Maybe U was—understandably—embarrassed by the obvious distraction of everyone in the room, because it wasn't long before he thanked me and Bane for the hospitality and made his escape with the excuse of going to the range for shooting practice. Jane went with him, but since Watkins was still there, Bane and Jon and I could hardly discuss the startling turn of events and Watkins was too polite to inquire. I topped up Watkins' wine glass and tried to put it out of my head.

"Watkins, why *did* you join EGD security?" I asked. *As sincerely well-meaning as anyone in EGD security gets* had been Lucas's assessment of Watkins.

Watkins's attention shifted abruptly from a framed photo of Lucas on the wall and back to me. He took a rather immoderate swig from his glass. "It's not a cheerful story, lassie." His tone was grim.

"I would really like to know."

He sighed, long and from the heart. "Well..." He hesitated, drank more wine, and finally began. "When I was at school, long time ago indeed, now, I fell in love. Bit like you and your young man, really, only... well, unfortunately for Cathie I was no Bane Verrall. She failed her Sorting, you see. Unexpected, like. I was heart-broken, of course.

"And I was a good boyfriend to her, or so I thought for fifty years or more, until you two showed me right up. Because I wrote to her, you see. Twice a week, for eighteen months, two weeks and three days. Refused to forget her, the way they wanted me to." He sighed again, even more heavily. "I think it was some comfort to her, though I can see now, decades too late, I should have done more. Dared more..."

"And after *that*, you joined *EGD security?*" Bane burst out incredulously.

Watkins smiled, thin and sad. "Something happened to her, in there. Someone did something to her. She never told me exactly what—knew it would have been censored, no doubt, even if she didn't want to spare me grief. But I could tell. So I swore then that I'd commit my life to making sure what happened to her never happened to any other reAssignee." He laughed bleakly, drained his glass and held it out with something so akin to desperation that I refilled it, though he'd had several glasses already.

"It seemed like a good idea when I was eighteen," he said, after another long drink. "Felt like I was *doing something.* I slowly figured out, of course, that I'd simply made myself part of the problem. Too late by then. Still, I didn't realize *quite how* ridiculous my youthful choices were until Bane here demonstrated how a devoted boyfriend ought to behave in such a situation. Makes me feel like there must've been a real shortage of devoted boyfriends for a very long time."

Bane shifted, embarrassed. "A shortage of dodgy Resistance contacts, more like," he said bluntly. "Which is hardly a bad thing."

"No?" said Watkins. "The results were pretty stunning."

"Not entirely," I said. "Not at the Facility. The helicopter pilot was killed, and it was only by God's good grace none of you guards shared his fate. And then there were the soldiers on the Channel Bridge..."

"Can't make an omelet without breaking eggs," said Watkins. "What we were doing was wrong, and any of us with an ounce of conscience knew it, however deeply buried the knowledge might be."

"But *you* were there because you wanted to help reAssignees," I objected. "And Sally, and some of the others..."

"At the beginning, yes. But once I'd figured out that what I was doing was just keeping the whole thing going, I probably should have left. But I didn't, because I needed a pay check. I was glad you didn't kill me, lassie, but I couldn't have said you were wrong if you had."

"Well, I would've," I said fiercely. "There was no *need* to kill you!"

Watkins shrugged. "Well, no *need,* no," he conceded, his attention straying back to the baby gurgling in Jon's lap.

Perhaps time to change the subject anyway. "Would you like to hold Luc?"

"Uh..." Warring emotions flitted across Watkins' face: disbelief, eagerness... closely followed by that familiar oh-no-what-if-I-drop-it expression...

"Here we go." I scooped Luc up and deposited him on Watkins' knees. "Just hold onto him so he doesn't fall off, but he can hold his head up fine so you don't need to worry about that."

Watkins' look of panic eased as Luc peered and cooed up at him, unphased. "Well, you're a dear little lad, aren't you?" he cooed back. "Goodness, this brings it back. My two were about this age when I first held them. Both born just when I'd gone back on shift, as my ill luck would have it..."

My two... But of course Watkins had children. EGD Security *officers* were exempt from the Stable Population Act since their higher pay and greater perks did not extend to much in the way of leave and even the EGD recognized that no one in their right mind would want to raise a family in a Facility—but EGD Security rankers, with their six months on, six months off shift patterns, were still expected to produce the regulation two children. So *of course* Watkins had children.

"Was it difficult, being away so much of the time?" I couldn't help asking.

Watkins grimaced and freed one hand from Luc, perfectly secure on his lap, to pick up his glass again. "They lived with their mother," he said bluntly. "It was a Stable Population match when I was thirty. We, er, did what was necessary, but we didn't take to each other. She allowed me access to begin with, then when the eldest was about five, she finally found out what I did for a living. I'd just said I was a security guard, you see, but it was too hard to hide the shift pattern and she figured it out.

"After a year and a bit, I managed to get access granted me by a court order. Once a month. Which in practice meant just six times a year. Judge was as prejudiced as the rest of the population. And Carol and David stopped wanting to see me once they got to be teenagers and realized all the stuff their mum had been saying about me was true. So my contact after that... was sporadic. I never quite lost touch, but..."

He drained his glass—then brightened slightly. "They've been in contact, you know, since those posts you wrote. So I really meant it, when I thanked you, y'know. And you making me look so nice in your book... I've seen more of them in the last year than in the last decade! Met my grandkids for the first time, as well." He broke off and pulled some faces at Luc, who was beginning to look disgruntled at the lack of attention, and Luc gurgled gleefully.

Bane reached over and tickled one tiny foot, making Luc giggle even harder. Our son was a happy baby.

"I don't know why they don't just give up on the whole Stable Population thing," said Bane. "All they'd have to do is lower the price of a third Child Permittance, and they'd have the same number of children without having to... you know, force people."

"They won't do it," said Jon, shaking his head. "The whole reason they came up with the Stable Population law was because they just weren't prepared to admit that the declining population the EGD had worked so hard to bring about was simply making the economic problems worse. So they came up with the excuse that everyone needed to have two children in order to maintain genetic diversity, but anyone with a brain knows the real reason."

"Well, they called it the *Stable Population* Act," snorted Watkins, slurring his words a little.

"Er, actually, it's called the Critical Genetic Diversity Act," I said, slightly apologetically. "Everyone just *calls* it the Stable Population Act because... well, because that's what it really is: their desperate attempt to put a brake on the population decline and at least keep it steady. Though they even now aren't prepared to go against their own ideology and let it increase again."

Watkins looked like he'd quite like to spit, only there wasn't anywhere to do it. "It's hard for me to say I wish the Act didn't exist," he said, quite heatedly, "because I wouldn't ever want to rub out Carol and David, however difficult things have been. But if it wasn't for them... Well, if it weren't for that *entire* stupid pack of breeding laws, Sorting, the whole bloody lot..." he was very red in the face now... "maybe Carol and David would have been *Cathie* and my kids. Suppose they wouldn't have been quite who they are but all the same... maybe... maybe we'd have had more than two... maybe Cathie and I would be retiring together... Seeing our kids regularly..."

His voice went thinner, almost... lonely. "Going to sleep at night with a clear conscience... We can't all wipe out our sins by firing squad... almost envy him in a way, you know..." He drank the last of his wine, though I was quite sure by now he'd had more than enough, and slammed the glass down rather hard on the floor. "Bloody EGD! Bloody EuroGov! You keep hammering them, lassie! You just keep hammering the whole pack of bleeding bastards! Kick 'em where it hurts! Yeah. Yeah..." he trailed off, staring at Lucas's picture again.

Bane eased Luc from Watkins's lap as he started fretting. "I think this little one is hungry *again*, Margo," he said... then pulled a face. "Ah, no, I think he needs changing. Oh well, my turn, I suppose."

He bore Luc off to the bathroom. Watkins was still staring at the photo.

"Did you like Lucas, Watkins?" I asked, remembering something Lucas had said. "Or just... you know, think he was a good superior to have around?"

Watkins' expression grew thoughtful. "Well now... when he first arrived, he was as nice a young man as you could hope to meet. As nice a young gentleman, I'd even say. Certainly I liked him. He kept order, but by the book. But then, after some years... Something happened. I never did know what. One day he was normal, the next... walking around like a zombie. Like someone had ripped his heart right out of him. He recovered a bit, to a degree... but it was like all that was left was bitterness and cynicism and... well, he got more imaginative with the punishments after that. I must say, they *were* more effective than the official versions."

"So... he never told you what happened?"

"No." Watkins shook his head. "He just changed overnight. To begin with... well, quite frankly I was afraid we'd have to break his door down one morning. Instead, a couple of weeks later he just jumped in the car and drove off, in the middle of the day, without saying anything to anyone. When he hadn't come back by the following morning, I suggested to Captain Wallis that she try the hospital first of all. Which she did. And he was there."

My eyes widened. "He'd tried to..." Surely not, Lucas had told me...

"No. It's what I *expected*, but no. But he *was* there. He'd been found lying on a garden path in the early hours of the morning, beaten half to death; two broken arms and a lot more. Well, if you do go out in your uniform without even taking a driver along... Officers are supposed to be driven around, you see," he informed me solemnly. "Supposed to make them look important, but it's for security too. It's a firm rule. He'd even take a driver when he took his plants into the forest. I often did it.

"Did you know that?" Watkins digressed, still slurring the words. "He used to take all the plants he didn't want to keep and plant them in the forest? Always a different spot. I asked him, why, once, and he said most of the plants wouldn't survive out there, and that's why he didn't want to go back. But he still planted them all, ever so carefully. Wanted to give them a chance.

"Anyway," he dragged his mind back to what he'd been saying with obvious effort. "After about a week someone called from the hospital and said we should now go and collect him and look after him at the Facility. But when we got there they didn't seem to know anything about the call. They were all too happy to let us take him, though. They weren't taking that good care of him, by the look of it. Hypocrites," he said loudly, beginning to get heated again. "Vile hypocrisy! *Vile...*"

Yeah, where did the organs the hospitals had been using come from, after all?

But seeing another rant forthcoming, I said hastily, "Did they catch the people who attacked him, or did the police not care either?"

"Well," Watkins blinked and took a moment to gather his thoughts. "Oh, well, that was odd. By all accounts the police interviewed him as they ought to. But he wouldn't tell them a thing. Just said over and over that he had no wish to press charges, thank you kindly. They gave up soon enough and cleared off. So no, I never found out who did it."

"How strange," remarked Jon.

22

"Yeah," I agreed.

Watkins shrugged. "Mysterious fellow, he was. I dare say you probably know more about it than me."

I shrugged as well. If Lucas hadn't told him, I didn't feel I could.

"How's things, Jon?" I said, since I'd not actually got around to asking yet. "How's the seminary?"

His face brightened. "Oh, it's great. Even just the things we've learned already... oh, it's fantastic, Margo; I'm loving it."

I smiled too. It was wonderful to see Jon looking so... happy. So content. If he didn't become a priest I'd be extremely surprised. "The black suits you."

Jon's cheeks reddened slightly. "To be honest, I feel very self-conscious," he confided. "At least, whenever I remember what I've got on. But that's why they start us wearing it so soon, of course. So by the time we're actually ordained—if we are—we're comfortable and can con-centrate on the job at hand, not what we're wearing."

"Yeah," I said. "It's a good plan."

Jon's head turned slightly in a familiar listening pose, then he winked in my direction and jerked his head towards Watkins. Ah, Watkins' head had tilted back against the sofa and he was breathing deeply and evenly, fast asleep.

"Well, thank goodness for that," I said under my breath. "If he'd left in that condition, think what he might have said to the EuroSoldiers on the way out?" Visiting Vatican State, he could get away with, nowadays. But tipsy or not, slagging off the EuroGov too publicly might get him arrested.

Jon grinned. "Yeah. Would have been fun to listen, though."

"Umm." I was feeling quite drowsy myself, after that nice lunch. Luc was sleeping through the night most of the time now, but he still woke us often enough to feel it.

"What did we miss?" Bane came back in, Luc asleep in his arms. "Ah..." he noticed our slumbering guest and sat on the other sofa instead. "Siesta time," he said more softly, arranging Luc in his lap. "Well, not for me, I'm holding the baby..."

Somehow, despite my determination to stay awake and talk to Jon some more, I woke up over an hour later to find Jon gone and Bane sitting with Luc still asleep on his lap, reading a book. Watkins was snoring slightly.

"Oh, Jon's gone," I said, disappointed.

"Well, this place being such a hive of activity," said Bane dryly. "He was thinking of joining U and Jane at the range, then realized that probably wasn't such a good idea." From his slight snigger, Bane had been the one to point that out.

"Can you believe it?" I said. "U asking Jane out! Perhaps it was... you know, just a phase for him, or... some issues that he's now worked through... So now..."

Bane frowned, though. "I don't think so," he said slowly. "Not for U. He told me once that his older brother figured it out way before him. He was fantastic about it, apparently, helped U so much. Kept him focused on how he was a child of God, how God loved him and wanted him, and he was no different in God's eyes because he felt those things, they were just temptations to be dealt with, the way everyone has temptations. I still hope his brother shows up alive."

"Not much chance of that by now, surely?" I said sadly. U's older brother had been a missionary in the EuroGov: far more dangerous even than a parish priest. No official EuroGov record of his execution had yet come to light, but he'd not turned up either, so...

Bane sighed. "No. I know. But anyway, what I'm saying is, I think Jane must just be... you know, that one girl in a million."

My turn to frown. "Then I really hope they're right for each other! Because if you're correct, U may not get another shot."

"Well, she looked pretty interested to me," smirked Bane.

Yes, she had, and small wonder. U was handsome, kind... and it couldn't hurt that he was Eduardo's unofficial heir, to boot.

Carefully, I eased off the sofa and went to join Bane—I really didn't want to wake Watkins until he'd slept it off a bit. From his snores he was still well out of it, though, so I turned to Bane eagerly. "Watkins was telling us that Lucas got beaten up and admitted to hospital. And from what he said—and the timing—Lucas must have been that EGD Security Officer Uncle Peter told us about!"

Bane frowned. "What, the one whose life he pretty much saved?"

"Yep."

Uncle Peter had trotted out the story now and then, usually in the context of forgiving one's enemies. It had always impressed me and drawn an ambiguous reaction from Bane. I could remember Uncle Peter telling it...

"I was visiting a dying parishioner every day in one particular ward," he would begin, "and I became aware of this new patient that everyone hated; fellow patients, nurses, doctors, everyone. He'd two of his arms in plaster and other injuries hidden from view; he was a mess. Hard to believe anyone could feel too harshly towards him, in that condition, but they did.

"I soon found out why; even my parishioner had no compassion for him—at least, not until we'd talked about it a bit. But this guy was an EGD Security Officer, one of society's ultimate scapegoats—you know they're even more reviled than the rankers. Someone had certainly had a pretty good go at beating him to death, by the look of it.

"The arms were his problem. He couldn't reach anything for himself. He was helpless. And the nurses who should have been feeding him kept leaving it for the next shift. Then the next shift would leave the job to the next shift. He literally was not getting any food or water.

"In partial defense of the medical staff, I don't think they were actually *trying* to kill him, but they were well on the way to doing so. To start with he had the bell button in his hand and he kept ringing it, but the way the nurses spoke to him! 'We'll get to you when we've time, stop bothering us,' was about the nicest thing I heard them say.

"Anyway, I had this feeling he didn't really want the food or water that much, he was just ringing that button out of some... I don't know, some sense of duty? Anyway, after a day or two of this, he'd had enough. I was there when it happened: a nurse came to tell him to *stop ringing that damn bell!* He asked for water—can't have had any for almost two days, and he was a sick man—but she just gave a particularly cutting response.

"Anyway, this was clearly the last straw. I'll never forget the look of total despair and exhaustion that settled on his face as the nurse left. He opened his hands and let the bell go. Flicked it right off the bed and closed his eyes, and I could tell he wasn't going to say another word. He was just going to lie there and die a horrible death from thirst.

"Well, regardless of his profession, I couldn't have that, so I went over and got the cup and put it to his lips. But he didn't want it, by then—if he'd ever really wanted it. He turned his face away and wouldn't drink.

So I said to him, "If you don't drink this water, you're killing yourself as surely as if you put a gun to your head." I'd not much hope he'd listen, to be honest. He looked that past caring. But you know, it had a remarkable effect on him. He opened his eyes and looked at me—such a look of anguish—and then he just started sipping, meek as you please.

"I came back after visiting some other patients and there was a stone-cold meal on his dresser, so I fed him that. And did the same whenever I was there for the next few days. He never said anything to me, so I didn't say much to him either. It was a dangerous thing I was doing, after all; exactly the sort of thing that might draw suspicion. But I'd no choice; I'm quite sure it was the only food and drink he was getting.

"Anyway, when he seemed, as far as my limited medical knowledge could judge, out of any serious danger from his injuries, I opened up his dresser drawer one day and found his wallet. He still didn't say anything, just watched me that way he did. I was worried by then that *he* suspected, even if no one else was paying much attention, but what could I do?

"Well, they'd put his security card safe in his wallet and sure enough, it had his Facility's phone number on it. So I phoned up the Facility and equivocated slightly by saying, 'I'm calling from the hospital' and that they should now come and collect him. Sure enough, they assumed it was an official call and along they came. Had to wheel him off in the bed, mind you, but no one cared. Suppose they thought it was worth losing a bed to be rid of him. Those ham-fisted but undoubtedly well-meaning guards were clearly going to look after him much better."

"Did he never say anything to you at all?" I would always ask, at this point.

"Just one thing. As they were wheeling him out, they passed me, at the bedside of old Jimmy, and he met my eyes for a moment and said..."

"Thank you?" Bane would suggest.

"Nope," Uncle Peter would say, grinning... then his face would sober. "No, not thank you. I think he'd rather I'd left him to die. No, he said, 'Don't worry.' Just that."

"What did he mean?" Bane would demand.

"I always took it to mean, 'Don't worry that I'm going to have you hauled before a judge to make a Divine Denial, Father Priest.' Or something like that. Anyway, I never saw him again. And I was never hauled before a judge."

Lucas had clearly kept his mouth as tightly shut about his unwanted savior as he had about the thugs who'd beaten him. I was glad in a way he'd never found out that Uncle Peter had died in his own Facility, albeit years later. Well, he'd know *now*, of course, but finding out in heaven was different. Impossible, surely to wring your hands and feel guilty when you're both radiantly happy in God's awesome presence?

"So who did it?" said Bane, much more interested in the old story than I'd ever seen him. "Who attacked him?"

I shrugged. "Could've been pretty much any thugs of any description. Practically everyone hates EGD Security, even racists."

"But why protect them? Why let them get away with it?"

I shrugged again. "I imagine he felt so guilty about his job, he considered that he deserved it. I can just see it."

Bane still looked doubtful. "You'd think he'd have wanted a gang that vicious taken off the street."

"I doubt his sense of civic responsibility was functioning at its best just then, Bane," I said dryly.

Bane's turn to shrug. "Well, perhaps."

Watkins' snores tailed off with a bit of a grunt. He raised his head and looked around, blinking and rubbing his eyes, then checked his watch. "Ah, sorry, lassie, how rude of me. Cluttering up your sofa all afternoon like some drunken sailor!"

I hid a smile. "It's no problem; I had rather a long nap myself. We'd hardly want to throw you out before you'd digested your dinner."

"You're very kind," said Watkins dryly. "But I know I drank too much, and I apologize. I'd better be on my way."

The worst effects of the wine did seem to have worn off, so after taking a group photo of the four of us for him to show his children and grandchildren, I took him back to St Peter's. There, Snail inspected his photos, deferring the granting of permission to me for any that showed Luc, Bane or myself, and then returned Watkins' EuroID card in exchange for the Vatican pass.

"Interesting company you're keeping," Snail remarked, once Watkins had headed off to finish his interrupted tour of the basilica.

"Watkins is a good guy," I said. "It was kind of nice to see him, actually."

"Kind of?" muttered Snail skeptically, settling himself in front of his screen again.

"Okay, so it's hard not to have mixed feelings," I admitted, then added firmly, "but I'm glad he came."

Snail spread his hands in surrender, so I headed home.

21ˢᵗ May (20)

Haven't written in this since last Sunday! Never mind. Had U and Jane to Sunday lunch again. No unexpected guests this time. They arrived looking decidedly pleased with each other. Besotted, you mean!

"We've told Eduardo," U announced, quietly radiant.

Clearly this had some special significance if you spoke VSS-ese, but I had to ask, "Er, told him what?"

"That we're..." he shot Jane a wondering look. "That we're... in a relationship."

"Oh. That's his business, is it?"

"Eduardo thinks everything is his business," snorted Bane.

U laughed at that. "This really is, actually. He doesn't like people to be on duty together. To prevent the distraction, you know?"

"Oh, right."

Jane caught my eye and beamed. Clearly things were going very well. Thank you, Lord, for that. Amen!

18ᵗʰ August (20)

Oh dear, I'm not doing very well with this diary. Three months since I've written anything. I'm just so busy with Luc and the blog and everything. I simply must do the hoovering this week. Bane keeps doing it, and he says he doesn't mind but I know he does really – and it's not like he hasn't got plenty to do himself!

> You know if I get really fed up I'll just stop doing it all, right?

Jane's just been here. Fretting whether U really likes her because they've been going out for three months and he's only just held her hand for the first time. I explained to her that for U, holding hands is pretty much the equivalent of French kissing for a less uber-chaste guy, and she cheered up.

I didn't actually say this to her, of course, but if U's holding her hand, I reckon he's made his mind up. Though he probably feels it's too soon to... well, to actually propose!

When she'd gone I did a happy dance all around the living room. *I can do it again, but only if you join in.* *I'm sorry I missed that!* *I'll think about it!*

I can't believe how much Jane is changing, though. She's so much less snappy and defensive nowadays. I kind of accidentally let slip something about that to U, and he just looked surprised. 'Well, isn't it obvious how starved she's been of love?' he said. I've been thinking about that quite a lot. And it's true, isn't it?

I always tried to make allowance for Jane's prickliness because I could tell how stressful her life must have been as an unRegistered child, always waiting for that knock on the door. But I hadn't really thought about how she must have felt about her parents. That they'd failed her before she was even born — and that they'd never made any plans to save her. She definitely loved *them*, because she didn't try to escape until after Sorting Day, when they could no longer be punished for it. But did she ever believe they really, truly loved *her?* Okay, most parents never made a run for it with their unRegistered child, but some did. And all... should've. Shouldn't they? *YES!*

I suppose I just feel bad that I was in the Facility with Jane for almost four months and I never saw what U saw almost straight away: that Jane is a much warmer, nicer person than I ever gave her credit for, if you can just peel away all those defensive layers. Clearly, as a judge of character, I suck. :C

Jane's an onion person — they're always hard to read. *What are you, a carrot? Totally straightforward?* *Well, you're an open book! Again!* *:-D*

25ᵗʰ October (20)

Luc walked for the first time today! On his own. Just a few steps, then Bane had to catch him! *So proud!*

Eduardo came to lunch. He suggested Bane might like to do USS basic training at last — Bane's been officially 'attached' to the VSS for ages – but Bane wasn't too keen. It's a one-year course and he can't see how he'll be able to keep the rescue missions going at the same pace if he's doing training all day and night. Especially with a toddler as well! As I pointed out. Eduardo didn't seem too bothered, just said true enough, we'll wait for a better time then. God's the only one who knows when that will be!

Bane was a bit at a loose end after the vote, having his eyes back, and everything, but it didn't take him long (precisely three weeks, actually!) to hit on the idea of helping star-crossed mixed race couples (like Juwan and Doms) to get out of the EuroBloc. Loads of them want to leave, so they can get married properly, and avoid the Stable Population Act forcing them to have kids with someone of their own race when they reach thirty unRegistered.

Strictly speaking, people can leave, of course, once they're Adults, but the EuroGov make it so complicated to actually get the necessary permits and visas and so on, that loads of people would rather just drop everything and do a runner, if they're sure they'll never want to go back. Bane calls it the 'Matrimonial Express' service, though of course no one is obliged to marry once they're safe in Africa. But most of them do. I get sent so much wedding cake!

Bane doesn't usually go on the missions himself, thank goodness. Even he can see that it's an unnecessary risk. Practically anyone else stands a good chance of getting away with it if caught, but Bane's still wanted on a few capital charges that the Vote didn't render void. He hates not going, of course. Ain't that the truth!   It's not the

He does go out to the ship quite often, mind you. same.
He's actually really good at playing the media angle. He

documents the missions and releases photos and non-classified info to the press. The public love the whole thing! It's really been fueling support for the campaign against the Breeding Laws — and a lot of the campaign is grass roots, as well, not just me!

The EuroGov can't lock you up for using the religious term 'marriage' any more, of course, but they still don't legally recognize religious marriages. People have to have a civil registration too. It's a minor point, but hopefully we might get to it one day. *Yeah, according to the EuroGov, we're not really 'married'! Idiots!*

26ᵗʰ December (21) *About time!*

U and Jane are engaged! U popped the question at this oh-so-romantic dinner on Christmas Eve. He took her along to the greenhouses, and he'd put candles and fairy lights everywhere in one of them, and a little table and two chairs, and they had a really private dinner, which is actually rather hard to achieve here! Jane was thrilled. She said yes, of course, so U is thrilled too. *Almost levitating,*

The only drawback of this long-awaited event *in fact!* is that Jane clearly won't be able to talk about anything other than wedding plans for the next year—or six months if she has her way. Don't get me wrong, I am really interested, but Jane is way more interested!

Oh, Bane and I are moving to a larger apartment soon, so Luc can have his own room. We'll still be in the same block, though. *I have this feeling we're going to be in this block for a long, long time - unless you can remove the target tattooed next to the scar on your forehead, anyway...*

17ᵗʰ June (21) *Yep.* *Bother, didn't realise it was that visible!*

I am such a useless diarist! I put bits and pieces from daily life into my blog, but never get around to opening this thing! However, I had to make an entry today. After a year's hard campaigning – and lots of 'Matrimonial Express' missions! – the EuroGov have just announced that, 'having become aware of serious concerns among the population' and 'as listening to such concerns is always our priority' they are instigating a 'temporary suspension of the Critical Genetic Diversity Act! So in future people like Watkins, or Juwan and Doms – or Unicorn, if he'd stayed in the EuroBloc – won't be forced to pair off with random strangers when they hit thirty! The main Breeding Laws are still in force, though, so Bane isn't out of a job yet. Am I allowed to write 'oh good', next to this?

Oh, the other big thing I wanted to record! Bane and I are hoping to have another baby soon. Luc is 17 months and needs a little brother or sister, don't you think? Definitely!

14ᵗʰ September (21)   Liar! ;-)
U and Jane got married today! What a wonderful day. I've never seen U happier and Jane was practically floating. She'd found a sort of deep cream and gold ball gown and she looked stunning. U had Bane, Snail and Bee for groomsmen. Jon and Kyle served at the altar. I was a bridesmaid, along with Jane's newest friends, Galena, Calla, and Kibuuka, a few of those rather rare things – female VSS agents! Plus Caroline and Harriet and Sarah. So loads of bridesmaids! And lots of the others from the Free Town of Kanju came as guests. It was brilliant seeing them all. I'm actually writing this the following day because the party went on rather a long time! As I said!

It was nice to catch up with Bee a bit, as well. They let him stay in the apartment with U, Jon and Snail to begin with, for familiarity, but after he'd been in his new job a while, he preferred to move to the Vatican Police Barracks. Easier being with his new comrades. Snail was a bit downcast about that, but he understood it was better for Bee.

They've remained best friends, mind you, despite Bee still not remembering more than a handful of things from before the nonLethal grenade. One memory he got back is of Snail, though, from their basic VSS training, and one is of his parents, which is really good since they're dead. But basically, Snail and Bee just carried right on being friends regardless of Bee's memories, or lack of, which just shows that some things go deeper than rational thought.

Luc is walking so well now! No baby news yet. Harder?

Good excuse to try even harder?
Why do we need an excuse?
Good point!

21ᵗ January (22)

Big news! The campaign has been growing, and Bane and I have certainly been doing all we can to help it. And now... the Race Breeding Laws are suspended! Pending further examination of new scientific discoveries that have recently come to light is how the EuroGov are putting it. Trying to make out that some new research is suggesting Genetic Mixes may not be the disasters for the human race that they've been claiming for so long.

Eduardo says if we keep this up the EuroGov may just wake up one day and find they've accidentally turned into a real democratic government! And that it's really not so bad? I suggested, but Eduardo snorted and said maybe. Or they'll panic, lose their heads entirely and start throwing their weight around, turn the place into a police state, people disappearing in the night, summary executions... like those dim-witted and therefore usually, in the scheme of things, fairly short-lived authoritarian states in the twenty-first century where they messed around with normal people's lives rather than letting them live quietly and making sure they had no motive to rebel, EuroGov-style.

Jon said surely not, that's never been the EuroGov's policy, they've always gone for clever and subtle with the main population, and they got their fingers singed badly enough when they resorted to force with the Vatican and with Malta that they're hardly likely to repeat the experiment any time soon. To say nothing of executing Lucas. I mean, yes, Lucas had been tried and sentenced to death already, and everything, but to do it in public like that. It was such a PR disaster, Reginald Hill got demoted over it, though sadly he regained his old position as Minister for Internal Affairs earlier this year. Well, you can't win them all, as they say. *Boo! Hiss!*

Anyway, to this Eduardo said okay, so they probably wouldn't go down that route, but we should avoid making them feel they're right up against a wall, because frightened people do stupid things, and very frightened people do very stupid things. He was looking at me at the time, so apparently it's my responsibility to pull the *Yes,* EuroGov's teeth so gently they don't freak out about it. *it is.* No pressure or anything. Thanks Eduardo. This latest victory can barely be attributed to me, you know! *Yes, it can!*

Bane said when everyone had gone, Yes! Now he can focus on helping families expecting a third child — yep, the non-racial parts of the Breeding Laws are still in force. The EuroGov levy such a large fine for the birth of a third child — several times the annual combined income of the couple — that most families feel they have to accept the free abortion. Especially since, with a baby on the way, even people who'd rather leave instead don't always have time to get the official travel papers through.

Bane was wanting to turn his attention to this before, but he held off because the Race campaign was gathering so much force. One thing at a time, don't split your energies, and all that. Because no one with a small child ever has enough energy. Fact.

Anyway, the more we think about it, the more thrilled we are that Bane can help these families at last. Especially because – it's big news all round! – I took a pregnancy test and – finally! – it's positive! Luc's little baby brother or sister is on the way! So we've got about 8 months to pray for more energy!

2nd March (22)

Kyle was ordained as deacon today! What a lovely Mass. All very nice.

When Kyle started seminary, of course they were still doing the highly pressurized four-year course, because of the desperate need for priests, what with them constantly getting executed. As soon as we won the Religious Freedom vote, they went back to a six-year course, because the four-year course was just insanely hard on the young men. They had about zero free time whatsoever, for four years.

Of course, six years is still pretty intense when most of them haven't been to university to get a head start, like they often had before the religious suppression began, but it's not quite so mad.

Anyway, Jon is doing the six-year course, but since Kyle and his year group had already done two years of hyper-pressurized study, they only had to do three more.

Felt like you were having a weeping competition with all those proud mothers, especially yours!
So a lot of them were ordained deacon today. I felt so proud of him! Of all of them.

It really wasn't good this year.

22ⁿᵈ March—Good Friday (22)

I can hardly write this, my hands keep shaking, and I just keep bursting into tears – I suppose that's mostly the baby's fault. But something terrible has happened. We were in St Peter's for the Good Friday service, and when I came out of my pew to go up to receive Communion this old man in the front seat of the public area stood up and started screaming at me.

"She's dead," he was screaming, "she died, and it would have been such a simple cure, all she needed was one organ but you put a stop to that, didn't you, you selfish irrational bitch, and now my Hilda's dead! She's dead and it's your fault, do you hear me!" And so on.

I didn't know what to do, whether I should try to speak to him, what on earth I could say... A couple of Swiss Guards were heading for the guy, they were keeping their voices down, of course, but I could just hear them trying to calm him, trying to get him to go somewhere quiet and talk to someone.

Then... everything happened so fast. I think one of the guards yelled, then U, who was bodyguarding me, dived into me, there was a shot, everyone started screaming and U was on top of me but his breathing had gone all gurgly and wrong but a load of other people jumped on top of us, including Bane, and wouldn't move until Eduardo gave the all clear and I kept yelling, "U's hurt, get a doctor!" but it seemed forever before they'd get off and let Doctor Frederick through.

Anyway, Doctor Frederick is still operating on U so we don't know much yet, other than that the bullet went into his chest, and he's still alive. I've never seen Jane cry before. I kept apologizing, I just couldn't stop, until finally she screamed that U was doing his job and she was proud of him and it was that bloody old man's fault, so shut up Margo or I'm going to slap your face! And I burst into tears yet again. Quite rightly.

At which point Bane insisted that I come home to rest for a while, for Baby's sake, so I made him stay with Jane. Sister Mari took Luc home for the night. And I am lying down on the bed but there's no way I can possibly sleep until I know if U's going to be okay, so I started writing this just for something to do.

Oh no, I'm crying again. But this is like Snakey all over again! Lord, please don't let U die! He put himself between me and that bullet just like Lucas once did! He was so brave, please don't let him die! Please don't let Jane be a widow! They're so happy!

~~What if~~ I just keep

23rd March – Easter Saturday (22)

I can't believe I fell asleep yesterday! I woke up in the middle of the night and Bane was asleep beside me, so I woke him up at once and asked about U. He said U was tucked up asleep in the hospital wing now. Doctor Frederick took the bullet out and got everything closed up and it wasn't too bad. Well, it was, because it was through the lung, but it wasn't, because it hadn't made a mess of anything else, so the recovery actually should be fairly straight-forward, even if it was immediately very life-threatening. Thanks be to God.

38

I was so relieved, of course I cried again. Hug, hug.

I found out this morning that the old man died. The guards didn't do anything wrong, they followed their protocols on who should fire at him and he only got hit three times, but he was too old and he died after a couple of hours, without ever waking up. That made me cry too. Honestly, Margo.

Bane was a bit less sympathetic about those tears. "Margo, he pulled out a pistol in the middle of a whole bunch of Swiss Guards and started firing it in the Holy Father's vicinity, that's not what you do if you want to live a long life. And might I point out, he was trying to kill you! Those who live by the sword, die by the sword, right? He asked for it." He really did!

"You missed the thing about him being deranged with grief, then?" I pointed out. I still think this is a good point.

"Lots of people lose loved ones, most of them don't It is. But— decide to go off and murder someone," Bane retorted.

"And if he was actually mentally ill?" OK, not so good.

Bane just scowled at that, and muttered something along the lines of 'Of course it would be better if the guy had lived to receive appropriate psychiatric care'. Eduardo's already looking into whether the EuroGov might have been — anonymously, no doubt — pushing this guy's buttons to aim him at me. I'd have thought that was rather far-fetched, only I know from that story Fox told me that they've done it at least once before, with another mentally ill man. He went after Pope Cornelius and also ended up dead, unfortunately, though for a different reason.

But the most important thing is that U is going to be okay! He'll be off work for months, but there'll be no long-term damage.

Thank you, Lord! AMEN!
                      AMEN!

19ᵗʰ April (22)

Okay, so I had a bit of a shock today. Mum and Dad are moving to Africa. They're going to head up a welcome center for the families Bane is helping. They just told us. 'Margo,' Mum said to me, 'It's been wonderful being here with you and Bane and Luc and Kyle, but we're far too young to retire and we feel a real calling to this work. We'll miss you all loads, but we can talk on the phone, and visit often. We'll definitely come over when the baby's due. Please don't be too upset.'

I'm not exactly upset; at least, not with them. I'm just shocked. I suppose it makes sense, though. They spent all those years running the Mass Centre; of course they need a proper project to throw themselves into. I'm going to really miss them, though, and so will Bane and Luc.
                                                    Yep.

3ʳᵈ July

Cutting and sticking again! This is a long one.

I was on my way to the Blessed Sacrament Chapel earlier (where Our Lord has been moved now that there are so many non-religious tourists traipsing round the rest of St Peters) hoping I would be able to stop worrying about the little one in my tummy long enough to actually focus on His presence.

Doctor Carol said that not all babies were as active as others and that as far as she could tell everything was fine, but still it's been bothering me. Luc, now running and chattering happily, had been such a placid baby, yet he was way more active than this in the womb. But surely Doctor Carol was right, surely it was just natural variation?

It was no good, worrying wasn't going to help and if I didn't stop I'd probably get weepy or something silly. My moods were like a yo-yo again...Tell me about it. No need!

Then I saw a lady sitting in one of the chairs, staring at St Peter's tomb and the baldacchino as though she wasn't really seeing them. She didn't look very happy, but that wasn't why I stopped. Lots of people come into churches when they feel unhappy, and the largest church in the world is no different. *You can just fit more of them in!*

I stopped because just for a moment I thought she was someone else, and it made my breath catch so painfully. Then I realized she was a she, not a he, and that it wasn't the last day and the dead hadn't risen. I couldn't make myself carry on past, though. I mean, surely, surely it couldn't be coincidence... *Nope!*

Eventually she became aware of me standing there, staring, and she looked up at me. And the words slipped out before I could get embarrassed about maybe being wrong. "Clara Everington? I mean... Clara Wherrick?"

She looked so shocked. Her lips formed the word, "How?" *Margaret Verrall officially knows everything...*

"I'm sorry; I didn't mean to startle you. You just... you look an awful lot like your brother."*...except gardening (& vacuuming.)*

I braced myself for rage, for a denial of having a brother, but although a spasm of anger crossed her face, her eyes remained haunted, and all she finally said was, "I know."

What was she doing here, almost exactly three years after Lucas had died? Surely she must be here because of him.

But I thought it more prudent to say, "Are you, uh, sightseeing?"

"Yes. Yes," she said very faintly. She looked up at St Peters as though seeing it for the first time. "It's... very impressive."

"It's beautiful," I said, then added cautiously, "Lucas loved it."

"I don't care about that!" she snapped.

"Right. Um, sorry. Uh, do you mind if I sit down for a minute?" She glanced at my belly and nodded uncertainly. I plunked down into a chair beside her with a sigh of relief. Baby might not be kicking me as hard or as often as I'd have liked but Baby still weighed plenty. "So, um, how are, er, Bill and Jilly?"

She looked shocked again, as though she'd not expected me to know the names of her husband—sorry, registered partner—and surviving child. "Fine," she said tersely, but added suddenly, "Jilly got Registered earlier this year. When they relaxed the breeding laws. She was in love with an Asian lad. Young man. Is in love." That came out rather defiantly.

"Oh, how wonderful!" I said. "I'm so glad the law got changed in time for her." Unlike Juwan and Doms... Sadness momentarily muted the joy at hearing that my work had contributed to the happiness of Lucas's beloved niece.

"Yes, I... Thank you for changing the law." She spoke awkwardly but with sincere feeling. "For several years, I've been dreading the heartache for her... for them both. The overturning of the Stable Population Act last summer was such a huge relief. But the collapse of the Racial Breeding Laws... we'd never dreamt that could happen! So thank you. It's a wonderful thing you've done for them."

My cheeks were getting burning hot. "It wasn't *just* me. Or even mostly me. Loads of people helped bring it about."

"You're Margaret Verrall," said Clara. "People listen to you."

I could only shrug. And blush. And change the subject. "Is Bill with you?"

"No. He said he wasn't stirring one step closer to that man, even if he was dead and rotted."

That man... Lucas. A flash of anger stabbed me unexpectedly and I fought it back. *Hormones, hormones...* Bill Wherrick had every right to hate the man who'd been in charge of the Facility where his son was murdered. As did Clara...

"Well... since you came all this way, would you like to...." *don't say 'pay your respects', Margo, just say...* "see the grave?"

She looked as surprised as Watkins had done at that suggestion, and her mouth opened in what was clearly going to be vehement refusal. Then closed. There was a long silence. I didn't break it.

Finally she said, "Since I'm here. I suppose I might as well. Then I can tell Bill I've seen with my own eyes that he's six feet under," she added harshly.

I was ready for the anger this time and thrust it down before there was any risk of it showing on my face. Just thinking about Lucas in my current state made me want to cry. Hearing someone speak like that was difficult.

"Right," I sighed, "I suppose that means I need to stand up again..."

I heaved myself up and led Clara to Security, where an agent I didn't know well went through the process of admitting her without any sign of concern. Soon enough, despite my seven-month belly slowing my pace, we stood beside the fuchsia-covered grave, Clara staring at the harsh headstone.

"It's what he wanted," I said quickly. "I'd have put something nicer, myself."

"Seems perfectly appropriate to me." Clara's voice was hard. But as she stood there, looking, there was a strange desolation in her eyes, as though only now did she truly believe something that she had known well enough for three years. That her brother was dead...

Still feeling a few tiny flickers of anger, I tried to imagine myself in her position. What if Kyle had done what Lucas had done? Lied to me, worked for the devil, and been complicit in Luc's death? My little Luc, not Clara's.

I shook my head, driving the imagining away. It was too painful. Even the thought brought tears to my eyes. I'd been badly at odds with Kyle for some horrible weeks once, and that'd been bad enough. Imagine if Kyle had died before we could make up. How helpless and grief-stricken would that have left me feeling?

And what if I had still been so angry with Kyle, if Bane had been so angry with him, that I couldn't even admit I was feeling any grief?

I smothered a sigh. *Lord, I really wanted to just have a little quiet time with you then go home and put my feet up, you know?*

Instead, I sank down on the stone bench to wait for Clara to finish eyeballing the grave, whiling away the time by giving Lucas a silent update on the progress of his plants. Since the communion of saints is all around us, he'd probably a better idea how they were doing than I had, but there we are.

And I'm really sorry but that yellow one did finally die. Even Ranulph couldn't do anything for it, I concluded. But almost immediately I added, *and please pray for your sister, Lucas. I'm sure you are, all the time, but please pray for me too. Pray I say the right thing, and don't send her storming off in a rage...*

Since Lucas had died only twelve days after his baptism, and I'd even seen him coming out of the confessional on the morning of the day he'd died, I didn't hesitate to appeal to him for prayers.

Oh, Clara had finished thinking... whatever she was thinking... and come to sit beside me. She didn't say anything, though, so I stayed silent. Hard enough for her to make sense of how she was feeling, surely, without me twittering on.

But eventually she did speak. "I swore I would hate that man until my dying day. But..." She fell silent again— eventually continued, "but it's taken me these last three years to realize that..." more silence... "that somewhere, in some crazy part of me, deep down, was this stupid belief that somehow, someday, we would..." Silence again. "That we'd be reconciled. Because he was my brother.

"When we were growing up," she shook her head to herself, "Oh, he was such a good brother. No one had a better brother in the history of the world. He worked so hard to spare me and mum. If he could physically have done everything, he would've. I used to feel ashamed of myself, once I was older, looking back on how much I let him do. How I sometimes took advantage of him, because I wanted to go out, or I simply didn't feel like doing some-thing I should have done myself. Because he'd do it, if I asked. He'd have done *anything* for me. For us..."

"He did..." I couldn't help putting in softly.

She gave me a sharp look, but simply went on, "It's a ridiculous feeling to have had. But I suppose it's why I came. I'm not really sure why I did. Even if he wasn't dead now, it would've been impossible. Ever. I don't know why I felt that way..."

"He's your brother," I said, even more softly.

"*Was* my brother, she said flatly, but without heat. "He's not been my brother for a decade and he never will be again!"

"Which is why you travelled over two thousand kilometers to come here?" The words slipped out.

This time the gaze she turned on me was furious. I spread my hands peaceably and shrugged. Her scowl, if anything, deepened, and she made a move as though to get up from the seat, and no doubt, march off out of the state.

I'd opened my mouth, groping for words that would make her stay, when Baby gave me such a good kick that Clara dropped momentarily from my mind as I rubbed my belly and crooned encouragement. "That's right, Baby, that's right. You get as much exercise as you need. Have a nice kick, have a nice wriggle. Get those muscles toned..."

Oh, Clara was still sitting beside me. "I'm sorry" I told her. "I didn't mean to ignore you. It's just, this baby hasn't been as active as Luc was, and it makes me worry. So I'm actually glad when Baby gives me a good wallop..." I trailed off, because her nostrils had gone pinched, and I knew what had done it.

"Why did you... name your baby after that man?" she asked haltingly. "I never did understand how you could do that."

"Because he was my friend," I said quietly, trying to choke back the grief that still welled up, even now. "And because despite all his terrible mistakes in life, at the time I knew him, he was a good man. Probably the most generous person I've ever met, and he gave my family an irreplaceable gift. Bane and I didn't even have to discuss it. When he died, we both knew we would name our son after him."

Clara was silent some more. "It's so hard," she said at last, almost to herself, "to think of him doing something good. As a boy, yes, but to think of him doing something good, *after*..."

45

"He found healing here," I told her. "He was adamant he didn't deserve to be happy, didn't deserve to be forgiven, and I suppose from a human point of view, he was right. But God has no time for that sort of human point of view and He forgave him anyway. Healed him anyway. Lucas found it a wonder, even after he'd accepted it'd really happened, so it's not surprising it seems strange to you."

"He killed my son," she whispered.

"No, he didn't," I said, almost as quietly. "That's exactly how he'd have put it, but no, he didn't. He was deeply complicit simply because of his position, but he was not the man who murdered your son. I suspect *my* husband killed *that* man four years ago."

That made Clara frown and go quiet for a long time. "You know," she said at last, "That never really registered before. That the dismantler who was killed during the escape..."

"Too busy hating Lucas?" I said matter-of-factly.

"Yes," she said, just as frankly. "I was. I was so glad he was going to be punished at last, I didn't even think about all the others."

"Well, there's no point hating them. Their lives have all been blighted by their poor choices." I couldn't help thinking of Sally and Watkins. "It's the EuroBloc Genetics Department who are really to blame for it all, and they're slowly getting cut down to size."

"You'd absolve EGD Security of all blame?"

"Not exactly, but hate destroys our future more than it destroys theirs."

"Hate is all I can ever have for that man."

I choked back a frustrated noise. All this and Lucas was still, 'that man'.

At a grumble from my stomach, I checked my watch. I was late for lunch. But I didn't want to let Clara go away like this, still hating and hurting. Whether God could reach her through anything I said, who knew, but I wanted to keep trying.

"Would you like to pop up to my apartment for a spot of lunch?" I said casually.

Uncertainty covered her face. No doubt she sensed why I wanted to keep her there, but however strenuously her conscious mind might deny it, she'd not come over two thousand kilometers, without Bill, just to look at St Peters.

"Well, um, thank you. That's kind of you."

This time, the guard had to get clearance from Eduardo before admitting a stranger, because of it being a secure block, but soon I was letting us in, hoping that the food was in a better condition than on Watkins' memorable visit. A visit which, come to think of it, was probably better left unmentioned.

"Bane, how's lunch?" Luc was in the playpen and Bane was at his desk, poring over something on his laptop. 'Stork' Mission plans? Hopefully not too dangerous, and hopefully not for *him*. The birth was so close now, after all...

"I turned the oven down," said Bane. "Well, when Luc reminded me," he added, shooting a grin over his shoulder, then turning around. "Oh, we have a visitor, I see." But a frown crossed his face as he looked properly at Clara.

"This is Clara Jameson-Wherrick, Bane." It probably wouldn't be very tactful to introduce her as Lucas's sister after everything she'd said so far, but I wasn't sure if Bane would remember Lucas's maternal surname had been Jameson, so I said, "Formerly Clara Jameson-Everington."

Bane's eyes widened. "Oh. I *thought*..." But he replaced what he'd been going to say with a welcoming smile. I had eventually given him a summary of Lucas's woeful history, since keeping something that big from him was a strain and I didn't think Lucas would mind, and he clearly guessed that Clara's brother might be a sore topic.

"Mama!" called Luc from his pen, so I went over to pick him up.

"You reminded Daddy about the lunch did you? You are a clever boy."

"Food burn-burn! Bad! All go ca-tee-ra!"

My heart gave a guilty twist at that. Clearly Luc had heard more of the row we'd had a few months back when his Daddy had let yet another meal burn than I thought. Bane had said he was sorry, but that it wasn't really fair for me to get so cross when he'd done it by *accident, and* since

I had barely touched the housework for months and Bane did have other stuff to do, too, you know.

Which was a very fair point, let's face it, but a very bad time to bring it up, and I'm ashamed to say I responded simply by yelling who cares about a bit of hoovering, Bane didn't seem to appreciate how hard *I* worked to make sure we could have some family meals when I had so many other things to be doing and would he rather we ate in the cafeteria ALL THE TIME?

Later we'd apologized a lot to each other and some good had come of it, because I'd been trying harder to do at least some of the housework and Bane was trying to treat minding the oven as a mission rather than a chore.

All the same, I couldn't help giving Bane a suspicious look. "You did turn it down *in time*, didn't you?"

Bane threw up his hands in a gesture of surrender. "Yes, it's fine. Anything even slightly well done is 'burn-burn', you know that!"

True. Well, only one way to find out. "Do make yourself at home, Clara. Take a seat. I just need to take a look in the oven..."

"Ye of little faith!" Bane called after me. As, Luc on my hip, I headed into the kitchen, I heard him say, "Would you like a drink or something?" so Clara was being looked after.

A quick peep in the oven proved that either Luc's excellent nose or Bane's new leaf had saved the food, so I took Luc back out to Bane, meaning to go back in and finish getting things ready. But...

"I can do it, Margo," said Bane, leaping up. "You stay with your guest..." From the speed with which he vanished into the kitchen, the thought of navigating a solo conversation with the angry sister of the man who had sacrificed his life to give Bane back his sight did not appeal to him.

I sat on the sofa with Clara, and put Luc on my knees, but he immediately tried to climb onto the fascinating new lap beside him.

"It's okay," said Clara, so I let him go.

"This is Lucas Mark, Clara," I said, avoiding the more distressing nickname. "Luc, this is your Auntie Clara. *Uh...* sort of," I backpedaled hastily. We always called Lucas

'Uncle Lucas' when we talked to Luc about him, so the honorary 'Auntie' had slipped out before I could think it through.

Clara looked deeply taken aback, but didn't fly into a rage, perhaps mollified by the 'sort of' qualification, not that Luc had registered it. "Antee Cla-cla," he giggled, reaching for her hair.

She gently detached him. "Well, you're a happy little thing, aren't you?" There was an endless sadness in her face, though, and it was clear enough she was remembering her own little boy. My heart twisted painfully within me, as unbidden, that comparison came back to me, of Kyle being responsible for the death of my little one. How could I ever forgive him?

With difficulty. Very great difficulty. But... the realization dawned... I *could*, couldn't I? By God's grace, I had forgiven *Father Mark* for exactly this...

My mouth had opened before I'd really taken the decision to speak. "Shortly before Lucas died, someone I'd known and loved dearly for years threw me down the stairs when I was pregnant." Clara's eyes widened in shock as I ploughed on, "He didn't do it deliberately, didn't intend it to happen—he wasn't in control of himself at the time, had no idea what he was doing: but he did it. I miscarried the baby—at least, I was a hundred percent certain I had at the time, which amounts to the same thing—and somehow I had to forgive him for what he did.

"Because, you see, he was someone who'd previously only ever sought to help me and do good to me. For some time I thought I couldn't forgive him, however hard I tried, but thankfully, I did manage to forgive him in time. Because he died, you see, a little while afterwards. And I can only imagine how difficult it would have been if I hadn't forgiven him before then."

Clara had listened with obvious sympathy, whilst Luc sucked happily on her beaded necklace, but as I reached my conclusion her face hardened. "You think this a direct comparison?" she demanded coldly. "Did your friend go around deliberately making women miscarry, and it was only with you that it was an accident that he would not have intended to happen? Or would you consider that all the other women's babies didn't matter, but only yours?"

"No, it's not a direct comparison," I said softly. "And *of course* all the other reAssignees matter. But it is *somewhat* comparable. Anyway, unless you were out campaigning for an end to Sorting, you were complicit in the *other* reAssignees' deaths, you and all of society, right along with Lucas and the guards. So in a sense it *is* only the... personal... death that *is* entirely..." I never got out the word *relevant*, because at that moment the rage in her eyes boiled over and she slapped me.

I gasped. She gasped too, and her hand went to her mouth, clearly so shocked with herself the rage had evaporated. Luc peered up at us both, eyes widening, mouth opening to wail...

Dragging a convincing smile onto my face, and trying to feel unconcerned about what had just happened, I snatched up Georg Friedrich's latest offering from the coffee table and opened the lid. "Here, Luc. Pre-lunch treat. Just don't tell Daddy..."

Luc brightened up immediately and reached out a little hand, selecting his favorite, a tiny apple-shaped marzipan. Friedrich made sure to put some of those in every time, regardless of what else he was sending. He did glance up at his 'Auntie' Clara, though, to check she was smiling as well. Her smile wasn't entirely convincing, but since he didn't know her very well he was satisfied and went to work on the little apple with single-minded concentration.

"I'm sorry," I said, trying to keep my voice light for Luc's sake. "Perhaps I shouldn't have said that." I'd pointed out that sort of thing on my blog so often, perhaps I'd forgotten how deep it could cut.

"I'm sorry," she echoed, keeping her voice light too, though it shook. "I shouldn't have done that. I expect you would like me to leave..." But her arms looped around Luc, as though, despite what had just happened, she didn't actually want to go...

"Of course not..." I started, but just then Bane swooped in with a heavy tray and started unloading it on the table.

"It's almost ready," he said, and thankfully went back into the kitchen without looking closely at either of us. My cheek felt hot, and probably looked red.

"It's fine," I told Clara, once he'd gone. "Would you like to use the little room or anything, before we eat?" She might like a moment in private to collect herself, if nothing else. She looked horribly shaken. In fact, whilst I didn't particularly appreciate being slapped, she looked far worse affected by the incident than me.

She handed Luc back, and headed for the bathroom when I pointed it out. Luc was still happily sucking on his fingers.

"What's he been eating?" asked Bane, appearing with another tray bearing the actual food.

"One of Friedrich's applelets," I admitted. "The conversation got a little bit... fraught... and I needed a distraction."

"Oh." But his eyes were lingering on the side of my face and his tone grew suspicious—and harder. "*How* fraught?"

"Everything's fine, Bane. I'll put Luc in his chair."

But Bane met me half-way to the table and took my chin in his hand, turning my head to look more closely at my cheek. "How fraught?" he demanded.

I gently removed his hand. "It was just a light slap, Bane. Listen, she was in a bit of a state before, if you ask me, though she was hiding it well, and now, she's pretty much distraught. So be nice, all right? And *say nothing.*"

Bane scowled, but headed back to the kitchen, which I took for assent. Sighing, I buckled Luc into his highchair. He giggled and clapped his hands, impatient for the meal to start.

Lord, I seem to be making a hash of this. Please help me to say what you want me to say, because I'm guessing I'm not. Clearly she doesn't go around slapping people normally—she went so white I thought she was going to pass out. But what do I say? Lucas, prayers, please? Uncle Peter, prayers? Father Mark?

We didn't talk about Lucas over lunch, though. Clara was very quiet and subdued—I tried to be cheerful and Bane made an effort too. She seemed a little calmer by the end of the meal—perhaps accepted by then that we weren't going to summon some scary Swiss Guards and have her arrested?—but she still seemed shaken.

I caught Bane's eye, glanced at Luc, and then at the front door. Bane's expression made it clear what he thought about leaving me alone with someone who'd already hit me once. Clara was still staring into the depths of her empty dessert dish, so I touched the place where my nonLee was holstered in reassurance and gave Bane a hard look.

He rolled his eyes and scooped up Luc. "I think we should go and visit Uncle Jon for a few hours, my little man."

Luc's delighted "Yaaaaaaay!" accompanied their departure.

"May I help you with the dishes?" asked Clara, still ultra-subdued.

"Oh, no, we won't worry about those now. Bane will help me with them later. In fact, he'll probably make me put my feet up, and do them himself. Shall I make us a coffee?"

By the time we were settled on the sofa with mugs of coffee, she was still showing little sign of recovering herself. Although I'd a feeling there was more to this than mere worry about having clouted the famous Margaret Verrall, I felt I should offer some reassurance.

"Don't worry about... y'know. We'll just forget it happened."

But if anything, when she looked up at me her face had gone even paler. "I... can't forget..." she whispered. "I... I haven't lost my temper like that since..." Her voice shook. "I've never hit anyone in my life, never. Except..." her voice wobbled and died.

A horrible, horrible thought inched into the corner of my mind. A thought that would explain a few mysteries.

"Lucas!" she blurted, as though it were something she couldn't hold in any more. "After Luc di... well, Lucas kept calling and begging me to forgive him, which was impossible, of course. Bill and I, we both agreed we couldn't stay anywhere near him so we arranged to move immediately.

We got it all organized in just a couple of weeks. Lucas phoned yet again on the day we were leaving, when we'd almost got the last things in the car, so I told him. Told him we were going and I never wanted to see him ever again.

"I thought it was too late for him to do anything, but you know how long it takes when you're going on a journey. All the last bits and pieces. Getting Jilly in the car. She didn't want to go. Just kept crying and asking for Luc. And if we go so far away, she said, how will Uncle Lucas come and see us? I told her we'd never be seeing him again but that just upset her even more.

"Anyway, the long and short of it was that by the time I had Jilly in the car, Lucas pulled up, still in his uniform—in his damned uniform!—and came rushing up the garden path, wanting to speak to me, wanting me to reconsider, to not go...

"I refused to listen to him at first, then I screamed at him... Heck, what a mess he looked, not himself at all... Crying... he was crying... In the end, he *begged*, on his knees, for forgiveness... I lost it then, I just lost it. I grabbed this spade—*his* spade, that he used when he visited, hence why we were leaving it behind—and I just started hitting him. Over and over. And he didn't fight back, he didn't try to defend himself at all. He could have stopped me, I know he could. But he just lay there, and I knew I could kill him and he would just let me do it. And I *wanted to*. I've never wanted anything more in my life. All I had to do was aim for his head, use the edge of the blade; I was so close I thought I couldn't stop myself...

"But Jilly was in the car. She'd already lost Luc. How could I make her watch me kill her beloved uncle? So eventually I managed to stop. I took the spade and put it in a black bag and squashed it in the boot, and we drove away. It started raining as we left, appropriately enough. I hoped he'd die. He was gravely hurt, right enough. I threw the spade into a river a hundred kilometers away and to stop Jilly hating me for what she'd seen, I told her that her Uncle Lucas had killed Luc, and that's why we were leaving. It was true... enough. She never talked about her Uncle Lucas again, and neither she nor Bill have ever mentioned what happened in the garden that evening. What they saw me do. And I never told anyone. Until now." She fell silent, breathing heavily as though she'd been running.

Okay, so I'd seen it coming, but it was still a bit of a shock. But it made perfect sense of everything. Of course Lucas hadn't waited for a driver, he must've been frantic, broken all the traffic laws to get there. Of course he hadn't been prepared to press charges. And of course he'd omitted this, when he told me his story. He'd loved his sister more than anything. About this, he had gone to his grave with his lips sealed.

"He never told me," I said quietly. "He never told me about this. He loved you too much."

For the first time, Clara looked as though she was on the verge of tears. Her voice was choked. "He... told you about Luc, though. Didn't he." It wasn't a question. It must be quite clear that he had.

"Yes, he did eventually. He... regarded himself as a dead man, you know. From the day Luc died, until the day he was baptized and received a new life. He couldn't forgive himself."

"Good," snapped Clara, though her voice still wobbled.

I'm not sure if it was the Holy Spirit prompting me, but I'd a feeling she still wasn't ready to forgive Lucas, and that if she got much more upset, she might just bolt.

I grabbed the photo album out from underneath Friedrich's box of confections. "I'm sorry, this is all very upsetting to talk about. Would you like to see some of Lucas Mark's baby photos?"

I opened the album and held it out—she accepted it rather automatically. But cooing over my little darling's snapshots definitely seemed to calm her, though it brought that sadness back into her eyes as well. But when she flicked further forward in the album, I was pretty sure that whether she would have admitted it to herself or not, she was looking for pictures of Lucas. She'd been alternately staring at and ignoring the photo of Lucas on the wall ever since she came in.

Well, if she got to the front of the album she wouldn't be disappointed. For my birthday, a couple of months after

Lucas's execution, our VSS friends had each devoted a bit of time to going through the old CCTV footage and putting together a collection of nice photos of Lucas—like the couple Eduardo had done immediately after it happened. It was surprising how many good ones they'd come up with. Not just shots of Lucas, or Lucas with me, but one of Lucas and Bane having tea, some of the Baptism party, and even one of the post-Baptism-party picnic. They'd put them into the first few pages of a nice new album—Jon's contribution—and I'd rarely been so pleased with a birthday present in my life.

Ah. Clara had just opened the album at the front page and gone still. She'd found what she was hunting for. She hesitated—I could almost see the battle going on inside her. Then she bent over the album, looking at the photos properly, slowly turning the pages.

Only when she made to turn to the final Lucas page, did something occur to me. "Oh, I'm not sure if you'll want to see..."

She turned the page regardless. The final double-spread was made up of several newspaper articles about the execution, complete with pictures, and a photograph-ically excellent photo of Lucas on his bier, taken by Brother Marcel, which had nonetheless been judged inappropriate to send to the media.

Clara didn't seem too disturbed by the clippings—perhaps in some hidden drawer at home, she had some similar ones—but she looked at the last picture for a long, long time. I often skipped these pages myself, though I wouldn't have wanted to get rid of them.

When Clara finally looked up from the photo, she kept the album open on her lap and said absolutely nothing. Her forefinger still rested gently on her brother's lifeless face.

Eventually I felt I had to say something, but found another apology rising to my lips. "I'm sorry about what I said before, about you being to blame for the other reAssignees' deaths. I only meant in the sense that *everyone* was to blame..."

"No..." Clara's voice was hollow. "You were right. I never tried to save any of them. Never tried to help them in any way. So Lucas was much more closely involved... but we were all allowing his wages to be paid through our taxes... You've been saying this on your blog for years. You said it over and over, before the vote. I just never... ever... somehow... actually applied it to... *me*." Her voice was shaking again.

"Almost *no one* did anything," I said softly. "I mean, the Underground were always vocal, outside the Bloc, and when I was growing up, I signed a few out-of-Bloc Human Rights groups' petitions, but nothing more. My parents ran a Mass center, I couldn't risk trouble, that was my excuse. But *everyone* had a good excuse. Children, poverty, elderly dependent relatives, or just a perfectly justifiable liking for being free and alive... Even the Resistance didn't do anything.

"But Lucas, Clara? His job was evil and wrong and deep down he knew it, just as everyone knew it. But with regard to *Luc*... well, if he'd known about Luc, he would have saved him, whatever job he had. Saved him or died trying. You must've known that. Why ever didn't you tell him?" It was the one thing I'd never been able to understand.

She shook her head violently, as though trying to fight off some unseen menace. Her eyes had gone wide, like a rabbit in the headlights, and she spoke very fast. "You just said it, he'd have saved him, *or died trying*... I didn't want to ruin my brother's life... even if he succeeded, everything he'd worked for, gone. He'd have had to start again in Africa, from scratch. We *all* would've...'

"But he'd have *rather* that, if it meant Luc had survived. *You'd* have rather that. Wouldn't you?"

Clara's face crumpled and she began to cry. To sob. Her whole body heaved as she choked and gasped in anguish. As though my words had punched through some dam inside her. It was quite alarming. I put an arm around her shoulders, rubbed her back, tried to comfort her, but I felt like a pebble facing down a storm surge.

Eventually, words began to squeeze through the pain. She was almost wailing. "I was so *scared!* I never told Lucas because I was *scared.* Of course he'd have saved Luc! I knew my brother! He'd have had him off to Africa—all of us off to Africa—just as soon as he could plan it and organize it! Nothing would have stopped him! But I was too *scared!* Scared of what we'd have to give up! Scared of the unknown! Scared of spending my life in some hot, dusty place, doing hot, boring work!

"It sounds so *stupid* now, but it was *hard.* It was hard to believe it would really happen, with Luc. When we were living so quietly, so happily, harming no one... How could it *happen?* To give up what we had for something totally unknown, far away in Africa...

"And what if it went *wrong?* They'd have executed Lucas, *maybe* not us, he'd have *tried* to arrange it to make it look like we didn't know he was spiriting Luc away, I'm sure, but even if that worked, they'd still have taken Jilly away from us, at the very least. How could I do that? Risk losing Jilly as well? To avoid something it was just so hard to believe was really, truly going to happen?

"But I *did* always kind of mean to tell Lucas, to let him solve my problems like he always had before, I did, but I put it off. Year after year, I put it off. No knock at the door, so what's the hurry? *Stupid, stupid!* Utter stupidity! By the time the knock came it was *too late!* Oh, why didn't I tell him? Why was I such a coward?"

She lurched to her feet, pushing me away, as though trying to flee something that clung all around her. She stumbled into the table and almost fell.

"You were right, Margaret Verrall!" she sobbed, doubled over a chair with her face almost in a dirty dessert dish, "You were right! My brother didn't kill my son! *I killed my son!* His *stupid, treacherous, cowardly mother* killed him! Then I blamed my brother for the rest of his life! Let him die thinking it was his fault! Let *our mother* die thinking it was his fault! Let her die hating him! But it was me! It was always me, I just couldn't face it! I couldn't!" She collapsed against the table and slid to the floor, whispering, "It was me... me, me, me..."

I couldn't help thinking she was now blaming herself as excessively as she'd previously blamed her brother, since there was another adult who must at the very least have acquiesced to not telling Lucas for over nine years, and who jolly well ought to have done something himself: Bill. But that didn't seem my business, and nor would it comfort her. But I didn't know what to say to her either.

After what she'd just revealed, my more judgmental side certainly wanted to agree with her litany: *stupid, treacherous, cowardly...*

How could she possibly have waited, put off acting, put off even telling her energetic, capable brother—serving, she believed, in the EuroArmy—when at any time the EGD could come for her son? If it had been my little Luc, I'd have waited only so long as it took to make the best and safest plan possible, and I'd have been gone. I'd have taken help from anyone who loved Luc enough to give it, too. It was still ultimately the EGD's fault, but she surely bore a heavy burden of responsibility for letting it happen.

Had Lucas figured out why she hadn't told him? He'd known her so well, surely he'd realized? Or had he been too mired in his own guilt? No, he must have thought about events from every possible angle over the years. Surely he'd understood her failure. And continued to blame only himself.

Clara was still sobbing in utter despair, but right then I didn't much feel like patting this selfish woman on the shoulder and saying, 'there, there'. But Uncle Peter's voice stirred in my memory. "Margo," he used to say, if I raged about someone or other's failings, "Not all people are as strong as others. You have to accept people as they are; love people as they are."

Clara was still Lucas's beloved sister, still a beloved child of God... And how many parents *had* actually summoned the courage to flee... or try to? Precious few. Her cowardice had not been an exception, it had been the norm. Even my parents had stayed, though their reasons for doing so were weightier—the Mass center, combined with the possibility that I might actually pass Sorting. But when I failed to return from school that day, they'd probably castigated themselves just as fiercely as Clara did now...

I crouched beside her, rubbed her back, spoke to her gently, but got no response. I tried a full hug, rocking her like a baby, but that had no effect either. She was distraught, and no wonder. The dreadful truth she'd suppressed so long was out of the bag now.

I sighed. I'd been so keen to get her to forgive Lucas. It'd never occurred to me that the cure might be worse than the disease. Still, in the long run it would be for the best, surely? You couldn't heal from something until you faced up to it. But she would need the right help and support...

Lord, what do I say to her? What do I say that will send her off in anything other than complete despair? Send her off with one modicum of hope? A sense of near-panic overwhelmed me. Lucas's 'duckling-syndrome' as I dubbed it, had allowed me to help *him*, but I was no counsellor.

"Me..." Clara still murmured brokenly. "*Me*..."

Me, me, me... I was being stupid about this. It wasn't all about me. Why should I think I had the experience to deal with this? *Thank you for that kick up the rump, Lord...* I went into the bedroom and closed the door quietly. Picked up the phone from the bedside table and dialed. I'd try the wisest person I knew, and if he wasn't available, work down from there.

"Sister Immanuella? I don't suppose there's any chance Pope Cornelius is free right now, is there?"

By the grace of God, Pope Cornelius had no actual meeting or engagement, and he put aside his other work to come and speak to Clara. I took my laptop into the bedroom to give them some privacy and tried to get on with a blog post. It was over an hour before Pope Cornelius tapped on the door and looked in, and I felt half-guilty at having asked him to come. But he just smiled, leaning on his walking stick and looking as calm as ever in his white papal robes, though he hadn't bothered to put actual shoes on before coming down and was still wearing his fluffy red slippers.

"Should we all have a spot of tea, Margaret?" he suggested. "If you're not too busy..."

If *I* wasn't too busy? An hour was an enormous expenditure of time for the Supreme Pontiff! "Of course," I said. "I have some cake. I'll put the kettle on."

Clara was now sitting on the sofa with a large, soggy papal handkerchief clenched in her hand. Her eyes were still very red, but she'd stopped crying and seemed much calmer. From her slightly awe-struck air, she had at some point figured out the identity of the vaguely familiar-looking priestly gentleman who'd simply introduced himself to her as 'Papa Cornelius'.

"I'm so sorry to be taking up your time like this," she said to me in a low voice when I appeared. Then glanced at Pope Cornelius. "Both of you..."

We murmured, "it's fine," and "don't mention it", and soon we were all settled comfortably with tea and cake. Clara definitely seemed a little brighter. The aura of despair and self-hatred that had enveloped her had cleared, and the thought of letting her walk away no longer filled me with dread. Even for a nonBeliever, Pope Cornelius's moral authority would have got through to her in a way nothing I said would have.

And she really had forgiven Lucas at last. At any rate, she told an anecdote about him from their childhood and didn't refer to him as 'that man' once.

Pope Cornelius excused himself after one cup of tea and one slice of cake and Clara clearly felt it was time she left as well.

"I'll send you a photo of Jilly's wedding," she said, after I'd given her my email address and an extension code that would persuade the VSS agents at the telephoneServer to put her call through to me.

"Yes, please do! And... one of Luc?" I said hesitantly.

Her face tightened, but she didn't break down again. "Yes. Yes, I will."

I noticed her gaze linger on the photo album where it lay on the table. Of course... "Would you like any of these photos? I can get more printed, so take as many as you like."

"Well..." Poorly-hidden eagerness in her eyes...

"Look, why don't you have the set? Seriously, I can get new ones printed, it's fine." I slipped all the Lucas photos out, hesitating over the last one.

"Yes, please," she said, almost inaudibly, so I slipped it out as well. I added one of Bane, Luc, and myself to the pile, found an envelope to put them in, and gave them to her. "Thank you," she said, then added under her breath, "Though how I'm going to explain these to Bill..."

What *was* she going to say to Bill after all this? Well, hopefully that had come up in her talk with Pope Cornelius.

"Do stay in touch," I told her, as we walked back to St Peter's.

"Yes," she said softly. "I think I will."

I watched her walk away over the marble floor, a small figure dwarfed by the immensity of the building—and her past—and offered up a heart-felt prayer for her continued healing. Then I tried to decide what to do with myself next. I felt exhausted, and would have welcomed a quiet sit down at home. But I also had a very powerful desire to have my own little Luc back in my arms.

No contest. I turned my steps towards Jon's apartment.

28th August (22) = big party!

Such a big day today! Kyle's ordination! Mum and Dad are here, of course. Kyle looks a bit dazed, really. In a happy way.

The sad part of this is that he'll be leaving, now. They're posting him to a parish in Africa, to be an assistant priest. It was judged too risky to send him into the EuroBloc. Eduardo doesn't think the High Committee would sanction an attack on him, either physically or legally — they're still working so hard to repair their image — but he doesn't quite trust Reginald Hill not to try something — an apparent accident, perhaps — and make it so convincing he doesn't get caught. Not a nice thought.

So Kyle's shipping out with Mum and Dad in a few days, and starting with a three month intensive course in the local language before going to his placement. He could get by with Latin with the Underground members, but there are people where he's going who aren't Believers, and he won't get far evangelizing them if he doesn't speak their tongue. It's all very exciting, but we'll miss having him around, and so will Luc. Umhmm.

17th October (22)

ALLELUIA!

Dominique Polly Verrall was born today! Hale and hearty, so it seems I was worrying for nothing! Luc is fascinated by her, and Bane is so pleased and proud of his little daughter he makes me laugh! She's the sweetest little thing! I feel really exhausted, to be honest. The labor was much shorter than with Luc, but if anything I feel more tired now it's over than I did then. Less adrenaline, maybe!

Never mind. Little Polly is well, and that's all that matters. I thought I'd find it easier this time but if anything I was even more worried! You held my hand very nicely!

6th December (23)

Would you like to see the bruises?
Sorry! Ha ha, you did all the work!

U and Jane are expecting a baby! They just told us at lunchtime! They'd invited Eduardo around too (also Jon, Calla Aguda, Kibuuka, and some of the others). Eduardo promptly sighed, rolled his eyes and said, "Looks like you're back to having Sister Krayj for bodyguard, Margaret." Yet again...

Poor Eduardo. Every time he trains up a few female agents for close protection work they marry some nice Swiss Guard or Vatican Policeman or fellow agent — not too surprisingly considering the choice! — and get pregnant.

62

Then he has to put them on desk work and whenever I need a 24/7 bodyguard Sister Krayj has to fill in.

Kibuuka has recently been snapped up by Fox — or vice versa? Anyway, if one is totally honest, she's quite a lot plainer than he is, but so *nice* I'm not sure he even notices! And Foxie has finally started to show an interest in getting that promotion to Corporal he needs before he can marry — and no one's in any doubt that a new arrival from the Polish Department called Zuzanna is the reason why! So Eduardo won't have Zuzanna on active duty for long, either, from the look of things!

Calla is still single, of course — she's becoming quite famous for it — but she doesn't want to do the close protection training. 'I'm sorry, Margo,' she says, whenever it's brought up, 'it's not that I don't like you, but I just worry, if it really came to it, whether I'd be brave enough to put myself in harm's way.'

But after Eduardo's reaction to the baby news: "You are so sexist!" Jane raged, waving the serving spoon at her boss. "Why can't I still bodyguard Margo once I'm a mother?" It was pretty funny, that!

"By all means re-apply for active duty once the baby's weaned," Eduardo told her ever so dryly, "If you still want to. But I won't hold my breath." And he glanced at U — quite clear what he was thinking. Almost two years on and U showed no ill effects now from his injury in the line of duty, but we all knew it had been a close call.

I knew what Eduardo meant, though. I certainly haven't felt like rushing into harm's way since I became a mother. Even Bane has been much more sensible about his safety since Luc was born, praise the Lord! And even more so now Polly is with us.

Did you just write my name and 'sensible' in the same sentence? Quick, print it out and frame it!

"Ah, yes," said Eduardo finally. "I believe I should say... congratulations." Well done, Sir. Top marks for the correct social response.   Bane, be nice! I was being nice!
He can't help it!

21ˢᵗ April (23)

"How's Georg Friedrich?" Eduardo asked me today, rather unexpectedly.

"Why... fine, I think," I told him. When Friedrich had persisted in sending me letters and edible gifts, I'd started writing back. It felt too rude not to. I was quite glad now, that I had. It was wonderful watching the hard, rather unloved and unloving tough-boy blossoming into someone more rounded, balanced, and... well, more human. I could still remember the paragraphs he'd written half in capitals, a year or so back.

"MRS VERRALL, YOU WONT BELIEVE WHAT HAPPENED EARLIER! THIS VISITING PRIEST EXPLAINED THE CRUCIFIXION THING TO US. I MEAN HE REALLY EXPLAINED IT! LIKE, ACTUALLY!   It's not a bad metaphor, actually.

"He used this metaphor about a man who loves the little birds in his garden loads and is sorry for them in the winter. He tries to get them to fly into his garage where it's nice and warm, but they've never been in there before and it's dark and they don't know what's inside, so they're too afraid to go in. So they stay outside and freeze to death. And the man thinks to himself, if only I could turn into a little bird and go into the garage and come back out again and so show them it is safe.

"AND THAT THAT'S EXACTLY WHY OUR LORD CAME DOWN AND BECAME A HUMAN AND DIED AND ROSE AGAIN! TO SHOW US THAT DEATH'S OKAY AND WE CAN TRUST GOD AND GO TO HIM!

AND IT MAKES SENSE, FINALLY! Okay, he said that's really only half of it, but that bit MAKES SENSE!

This moment of conversion had been a long time coming, but since then Friedrich seemed to have developed a genuine faith, and it had done him a world of good.

"He's really excited, actually," I told Eduardo. "His third review is coming up, and you know the third review is the first time they can potentially be released, or transfer to a semi-secure work placement. I think he's got a good chance, actually."

Friedrich was in for murder, albeit with some extenuating circumstances – i.e. criminal orders from his superiors – and had only done four years, but the farm took a very fluid approach to sentences – in fact, no exact terms were specified. The actual state of a person's rehabilitation was what mattered, and they had lots of clever tests and psychiatrists to weed out the fakers. But I didn't think Friedrich was faking.

"I think he has a good chance too," said Eduardo. "They've been trying to persuade him to direct his thoughts to a cookery career, but he won't bite. Just wants to join the VSS and be your bodyguard."

That wasn't news. His ambition hadn't wavered as the years passed.

"Anyway," went on Eduardo, "As you know, I'm off to Africa to tour the Free Towns and do a security overview, so I thought I might drop in on Friedrich and see what I think of him. It does sound like he's a reformed character. What do you think?" Why so interested, Eduardo?

"Me? Oh, he's reformed all right. That narrow escape from Dismantling did the job, no mistake."

65

Once Eduardo had gone it occurred to me I hadn't asked him *why* he wanted to see Friedrich. Oh well.

My question exactly!

9th June (23)

Jane's had her little boy! They've named him Arthur Jayesh after U's brother and Jane's brother. He's the most darling little thing. U thinks he looks really like Jane but I think he looks a lot like U, too. And yes, there's a lot of 'he looks like U' jokes going on!

Jane's already told me if I say that to her one more time she's going to slap me!

2nd August (23)

Okay, so I was walking down the corridor earlier and who should I meet but Georg Friedrich! Well, Eduardo did say yesterday that he needed a word, but I was too busy to call him. Friedrich came rushing over and I kid you not, got down on his knees and I think he was aiming at kissing my feet, but I managed to get him up before he could do it. He kept saying, "I swore I would! First time I saw you! Should have done it before!" But I managed to dissuade him. Told him to find a statue of Our Lord and kiss his feet instead.

Anyway, it seems – and I got this from Friedrich since I had neglected to phone Eduardo – that Friedrich's been released onto a six-month work placement in Vatican State with a view to maybe applying to the Vatican Police at the end of it. Apparently Eduardo told him not to apply straight to VSS because he'd be turned down, but to apply to the Vatican Police, then, if he got in, to do a year or two there and prove himself before applying to VSS. So it sounds like Eduardo's almost... encouraging him?

Grrr!

Bane got angry when I told him and phoned Eduardo and yelled at him, crosser than I've seen him for years. "I know he's turned into a half-way decent guy; I read his letters!" he bellowed. "But he still tried to kill Margo, or have you forgotten? And you really want him to be her bodyguard?"

I so wanted to punch him!

"Bane," said Eduardo, in a very patient voice (Bane had it on the speaker setting) "Friedrich has already had comprehensive military training, including special ops. And there are compelling reasons to believe in his sincerity and loyalty. Of course I'm pleased he still wants the job, and if you care about Margaret's safety, you should be too. Margaret saved his life, remember. And because of that Friedrich would like nothing better than a chance to put himself between her and certain death, whatever the risk to himself.

"Why do you think I don't push Calla to become a bodyguard?" he went on. "Because she doesn't have the necessary level of conviction that saving Margaret is important — you know, important quite aside from the simple fact that Margaret is nice and doesn't deserve to be assassinated — and nor does she have the even more effective motivation of deep personal gratitude. Why do you think Jane is such a good bodyguard, and why she may very well come back to it, baby or not?"

Bane growled a bit, but calmed down and went to pick up Polly, who was looking decidedly put out by all this shouting. I just stood, my cheeks burning. Jane had never broadcast her motivation the way Friedrich did, but now Eduardo mentioned it — she had been awfully keen to get on the close protection course as soon as possible, a course which would inevitably lead to her being detailed to guard me, since I was one of the most protected female residents of the state... Well, I had saved her life.

But it was still embarrassing to think she might be so focused on protecting me.

Anyway, it looks like Friedrich is here to stay. I suppose I'd better invite him to dinner. Groan!

I hope Eduardo has warned him not to stir one step out of the Vatican State. Though I'm sure Friedrich can figure that out for himself. The EuroGov are still busy executing people. I haven't got much traction with my campaign against that so far. Now that Sorting and Religious Suppression have ended, it's just criminals and Resistance fighters being executed, and people just aren't that bothered. It makes me so angry, though.

Okay, so the EuroBloc isn't as wealthy as back in the twenty-first century, nowhere is, but as if they can't 'render one who has committed an offense incapable of doing harm' through nonLethal means like, ooh, let me see, tracking chips and work programs, or for the most dangerous offenders, prison! Just like other Blocs do! They don't need to kill!

I'd have liked to prioritize this more, but I've had to do the same as Bane and put it on the back burner slightly in order to focus on the Breeding Laws. The Breeding Laws are, after all, affecting innocent people. But I'm not giving up. The Church's teaching is perfectly clear on this, not that the EuroGov care about that, and it has been for over a hundred years: 'Today ... the cases in which the execution of the offender is an absolute necessity "are very rare, if not practically nonexistent."' No absolute necessity in the EuroBloc today, no sir!

I think I will mention to Friedrich about not putting so much as a toe over that white line, though. I'm sure I don't need to say it, but... well, I can never forget what

happened to Lucas, and Friedrich's under sentence of
death just the same as Lucas was.
I doubt he's forgotten!
Relax!

6th October (23)
The kind I like!

So, big news! Good news, though a bit sooner than
intended. We're having another baby! My fault, actually.
Last month Bane was going off on his first risky mission
since Polly was born and I did have a few returning signs
of fertility but I was like, oh, I'm still weaning Polly, it'll
be fine. Definitely a case of famous last words, though
fortunately in a really delightful way! *Yep!*

We haven't told anyone yet, of course, except Doctor
Carol. The baby's due in the summer. Luc will be delighted,
he liked holding Polly so much when she was little, but
she's too big for him to manage now! Another little
brother or sister to cuddle will make him very happy!

On the subject of Luc, Bane's been teaching him to
say the rosary. How wonderful, you might think. Well, to
be fair Bane says he just said the alternative version as a
joke, and oops, it stuck (though he thinks it's hilarious,
mind you!). Anyway, now when we say the rosary as a
family, this little voice keeps saying, "Hail Mary, full of
Grace, punch the devil in the face."
Come on, admit it, Margo, it IS
hilarious!

18th January (24)
Maybe!

Maybe I should just give up on this diary! I write so
little in it. But I've been meaning to note that Friedrich
has been accepted into the Vatican Police. Is he chuffed
or what? I've never seen a uniform so carefully ironed.
Every time I see him it's pristine.
*I really want to make a derogatory comment here, but I
find I actually quite like him (how is this even possible?),
so I s'pose I won't.*
*I should think not! Friedrich thinks you're the second-best thing
since sliced bread, you know that!*

69

He came round to show us when he first got it. Luc wanted to know whether Uncle Georg would still have time to make him marzipan animals — he prefers animals to apples now. Friedrich promised most solemnly that Luc's supply wouldn't suffer, so Luc was happy for him as well.

Children's priorities are so uncomplicated!

14th June (24) ALLELUIA!

Javier Luciano has arrived! He made his intentions known on the night of the 13th, actually, but my goodness, it took ages this time! I was so glad when he was finally with us. Luc's overjoyed to have a little brother, though Polly clearly doesn't know quite what to make of little Javi. *I swear it gets worse each time! Do NOT let me listen to any more of Doctor Carol's medical horror stories!*

I never got around to mentioning that Jane's pregnant again. Fuming because Eduardo's stuck her back behind a desk once more. She did get back on active service again after Arthur was born, surprisingly quickly, and she swears she'll do it again. Everyone believes her this time! *And they'll hardly dare admit it to her face if they don't!*

15th July (24)

Javi baptized today — by Kyle! He was able to come home for a visit. He's ever so brown, and loving Africa. He doesn't see as much of Mum and Dad as you might think, because Africa is so huge and they live in totally different places. Doh! *Excuse me? You looked surprised too! I was. Just couldn't resist!*

12th September (24)

Yippee-hooray!

First big political breakthrough for two years! The EuroGov have just announced that all couples will be allowed three children. Finally! But the exorbitant fees for Fourth Child Permittances will remain in force, along with the pressure to abort. So Bane's not out of a job yet! He says when there are no more people wanting assistance to leave the EuroGov, he'll take over Lucas's greenhouse and become a gardener — because he reckons he'll be too old for much else, by then! It's probably true!

Actually, I think he's a little more serious about that than he lets on. He looks after the plants, now, and sometimes takes Luc down to the greenhouse for lessons from Ranulph. I've suspected for some time that he is slowly developing a genuine interest. Lucas would be thrilled!

Perhaps I've just had all I can take of watching you sobbing over dead plants.

15th November (25)

Almarda Matilda born. U and Jane ecstatic! What a darling little girl. Very sweet. Time for a new round of 'U'

And we're moving again! Three bed apartment   jokes! this time, same block, of course. Feels like only about thirty seconds since the last move! 15 seconds.

19th February (25)

Well, 'Uncle Georg' has done it at last. Just been accepted for VSS basic training. He celebrated by throwing a chocolate party! Chocolate cake, chocolate truffles, chocolate puddings... Everyone was angling for an invite, and I mean everyone!   All wanting you to put in a good word for them!

Ferrari's little daughter Jasmine got one, and he and Galena were trying to be so adult about who was going to accompany her. 'You should go, dear.' 'No, you go, dear.' Friedrich solved it by saying, "Oh, of course you can both come"!
                                                    Very wise.
Pope Cornelius forbade anyone to photograph him at the event — he didn't want pictures online of him with

chocolate all over his face just like all the children. Though we all looked the same by the end! *I've certainly got some great pics of you and the children!*

23rd January (26)
Okay, almost a year since I wrote in this diary! I am quite seriously thinking of giving up on it. I put so much stuff on my blog, it seems a bit of a waste of time. I won't get rid of it, of course. I'll just fill it up with other stuff. I've put quite a lot of things in the back already. *So have I!*

Ditto.

But anyway, something serious to record. *Dear* Father Mario died a couple of days ago. He made such a good recovery from his heart attack after the Battle for the Vatican, it sometimes felt like he would go on forever. But he had a terminal diagnosis three months ago. We'd have ~~liked~~ *keep him forever.* to

He wasn't bothered. Kept telling Luc and Polly that they should be envious of him, because he was off to heaven to be with God and lots of people he loved. He was bed-ridden for almost two months and Luc and Polly went to see him loads. *Definitely the way I want to go.*

Anyway, he died so peacefully and prayerfully that's why I called it serious news, not sad. Because although we all miss him, in a way it was a really happy event.

I wish someone could explain that to the doves, though. They're still lined up on Father Mario's hospital room window ledge, cooing mournfully for him. :(
Making Nurse Poppy cry and driving Doctor Frederick mad!

4th February (26)
Go Jon!
Jon was ordained Deacon today. But if anyone talks about his ordination to the priesthood (which no one doubts will follow) he's still all like, 'if the Lord wills', 'if

I'm judged suitable'. Which isn't wrong, of course, but he's so humble, it's lovely. *Jon, humble? I'd never noticed.*

We had a big party for him. He's worked so hard. The studying is so much more difficult for him, and takes up so much more time. I forgot to record that Eduardo — or rather, Erik, one of his tech guys, whose main job is to work for Jon — adapted some ancient software to make it run on modern computers, so that Jon could have the computer read him the texts, or print it on the Braille printer he's developed with Erik's help. They've even come up with a Braille keyboard. *Which I do not need: thank you, Lucas.*

Because as well as studying, can you believe it, he's been heading up the 'Imaginary Limits' Foundation, which has been developing and propagating all kinds of technology to help those with disabilities. Even some departments of the EuroGov are collaborating with them. *That is v. cool.*

He wants to go on an extended visit to Africa, and go all around and study some of the methods they're using there. Some of them aren't so high tech, but are very effective. He hasn't got time to do that until he's ordained, though, after which it's looking likely he'll be assigned to the Foundation permanently.

25th February (26) *Sooo disappointed he didn't get to die for you yet! Bane! NOT funny!*
Friedrich was on duty for the first time today. Like having a particularly paranoid cat winding around my ankles all the time. I hope he'll calm down. Okay, the odd person is always getting picked up trying to enter St Peter's with a knife (or even a gun, last month), though not all of them will admit who they're after (some of them are foaming-at-the-mouth type atheists who want

73

Pope Cornelius, I'm afraid) – but it's been two years since anyone *actually* got close enough to me to try anything.

Oh, I think I forgot to write anything about that last assassination attempt in here. I was doing an informal Q&A and discussion group by the colonnades in St Peter's Square and a man pulled a knife on me. Jane's quick reaction saved me – she broke his wrist and took his knife and a really big agent called Kugande promptly flattened him.

At that point he started screaming about some lost loved one, like the old man, but Eduardo looked into it and he's a street criminal who doesn't appear to have lost anyone close to him, so Eduardo thinks Reginald Hill simply paid the guy to preferably kill me, but at least to cause trouble. One day he's going to get his comeuppance. Or more likely a come-down-ance! Repent, Regi, you evil rat!

The EuroGov are busy collecting sob stories about 'hard cases' where someone has actually died who would have lived when Sorting was still around. People aren't paying much attention so far – they're all pleasantly surprised by the range of alternative treatments that exist, I think – but we mustn't become complacent. I do worry that if anything happens to someone too high profile, it could stir up public sympathy. That worries me too.

Or, I suppose, if grief-stricken people keep appearing on the news, trying to kill me. Even if people disapprove of attempted murder, that apparent level of grief makes the abolition of Sorting look bad. So I suppose I shouldn't be complacent about *that*, either. I do still need Friedrich and the others. Sometimes I wonder if I'm going to have to have a bodyguard for the rest of my life. That makes me feel tired.

It makes _me_ want to go and bump off Evil Regi. Bane!

Wouldn't you just love it if the guy dropped dead, Joke! (Well, just-about...) Hmm.
though? Be honest...

DROPPED dead, yes! Assassinated by an angry rival, yes! That's different! 74 Even *better* if he repented first!

25ᵗʰ June (26)   *Prayers for energy starting now.*
Well, I had to record this! Baby number four on the
way. Bane over the moon. Luc and Javi are pleased, Polly
is sulking. But she loves Javi to bits now, so hopefully she'll
come round. Baby due in the New Year.

Mum and Dad asked if we wouldn't like to move to
Africa, now there isn't quite such a need for us to be
right here. Bane and I talked it over, but we agree it's
better if we stay. Better for his work, and for mine. And
at the end of the day, perhaps the real reason is simply
that this is our home. We don't want to leave. *Nope.*

We ran it past Luc and Polly, and they hated the
idea. In fact Polly then cried for about an hour because
she was afraid we would ignore her opinion and whisk
her away the way Ferrari did with her friend Jasmine a
few months ago. Galena always wanted to farm, it turns
out, and Ferrari was up for it. Anyway, Jasmine's actually
loving Africa now, but Polly won't believe that! We
eventually convinced her we really weren't going, anyway.
Phew. *Phew!*

7ᵗʰ July (26)   *How cool does that sound?*
So as of today, Jon is now 'Father Jonathan Revan'.
The Ordination Mass was wonderful. It was so good to
see all those young men giving their lives to the Lord —
though (hopefully) in not quite so literal a way as in the
bad old days, thank goodness. Jon looked so happy. *Yep!*

Luc announced afterwards that he's going to be a
priest when he grows up, like Uncle Jon and Uncle Kyle
and Uncle Peter and Uncle Mark and Uncle Cornelius
and... Well, we had to stop him eventually because it was
time for the photographs! *Father Lucas Verrall?*
Ha ha, getting a bit ahead of yourself, aren't you, Bane?
That would be cool, though.
Certainly would.

75

The sad part of this ordination is that Jon is now off to Africa. But only for six months, so it's not that bad! He's very excited, as you can imagine. Polly wants him to bring her back an 'African Hamster' from her Auntie Harriet's breeding farm, despite the fact I keep explaining to her about how the poor thing would spend one sixth of its entire life in quarantine. Jon is more cunning than I am: he just says he'll see whether any suitable ones are ready to leave their mother when he calls in there. Which there won't be.

11th September (26)

I had to record what's been going on recently. It started on the eleventh. We were all at the breakfast table when there was a tap at the door and a call of "Post". Luc leapt up and ran to get it, though we've told him time and again that Bane or I should answer the door. Hard to believe he'll be seven in four months! Practically impossible!

It was indeed the post and not an assassin, and Luc came swooping back to the table with his arms spread like wings, 'landed' on his chair and gave quite a good owl hoot. (He's been reading some children's classics where owls deliver post and now he wants to be an owl every morning. We're delighted with his reading level, even if it does wreak havoc with our security procedures.)

"Here you go, Mummy," he said, after sorting quickly. "Here you go, Daddy."

"Thank you, little owl," said Bane solemnly.

"Thanks," I said, accepting the larger pile, then noting Javi's look of silent unhappiness. "Polly, that's Javi's toast. Give it back and I'll butter you another slice."

"I'll do it!" Luc seized another piece of toast and started buttering. "Jam or honey, Polly?"

"Both!"

"You can't have both. You've got to pick!"

"You're mean! Mummy, Luc's being *mean!*"

76

"He's not being mean; he's buttering your toast for you after you stole Javi's. What do you want on it, jam or honey?"

"Both!"

"Or *neither?*"

Polly stuck out her lower lip and pouted at me. "Jam!"

"Well, ask Luc nicely, come on, Polly..."

Polly glared at Luc instead. "Jam, *please.*"

Luc was already spreading jam on the toast with sunny enthusiasm. He was still a happy, good-natured boy. Polly, alas, was willful at the best of times, and downright horrible first thing in the morning, though hopefully she'd grow out of that. Javi, thank the Lord, was more in Luc's mold, though less emotional. If Luc or Polly had lost their toast when they were two, they'd have wailed full out, but Javi took everything very calmly. Right now he was placidly pulling pieces off his restored toast and putting them into his mouth with the unhurried air of one who has total confidence in their food supply despite recent disruption.

Polly was starting on her new slice of toast and Luc was tucking back into his own food, so I took a bite of my own and flicked through my pile of letters. Most went onto a larger 'fan' mail pile, which I would open and read, then pass on to Sister Mari and her team.

But I put aside a couple with the postmark of African Free State governments, one from my mum, another with the address of a major New York media corporation printed on the back, and one from Clara Everington. I always read Clara's letters in private before sharing them with the children since they varied between sunny updates on her grandchildren and depressive rants unsuitable for Luc's and Polly's ears. Though the grim letters were very much in the minority nowadays, thankfully.

I took another few bites of toast, opened the New York letter and choked. Oh good grief. They wanted to make a TV series about me. Some young up-and-coming actress would play my New Adult self, they just wanted me on the production team for authenticity's sake, a few interviews for publicity... Argh, no, no, no. I so wasn't interested. Unfortunately, Eduardo had already seen this and I could hear him and Pope Cornelius already, telling me how good it would be for the cause...

Now that the public's enthusiasm and interest had begun to wane with the passing years, the EuroGov were starting to push back wherever they could. A dramatized series reliving the glory days of the Liberations and the Vote could only do good. All the same, I stuffed the letter back into the envelope, slid it onto the bottom of the pile, and gulped water.

"Are you okay, Mummy?"

"Fine, Luc. Toast went down the wrong way."

"Mummy, Daddy, I've been thinking, if it's a girl... we should call her Hedwig! There's a Saint Hedwig. What do you think?"

"Er..." I said.

"No," said Bane, ripping open another letter.

"Awww," said Luc. "Mummy likes it!"

"Er," I said again.

"Actually, in this case I am quite confident in translating 'er' as meaning, *no*," said Bane.

"Mummy?" challenged Luc.

"Sorry, darling," I said. "Er does mean no, in this case. We were thinking more along the lines of Helen, after your great-grandma."

Luc sighed heavily. "Well, Helen isn't *terrible*, I suppose." He brightened. "If it's a boy, can we call him Norbert? There's a statue of Saint Norbert in St Peter's—you know, Uncle Lucas's favorite..."

"If it's a boy, we're calling him François," I said firmly. "We've decided that."

Luc sighed again, and gobbled up the last of his toast. I glanced at Javi, but he was still competently munching. I took another bite myself and picked up my mum's letter, then looked up at Bane as some subliminal voice raised the alarm. He was staring at what he held with a look more appropriate for a ghost than an envelope.

"Bane?" I said, keeping my voice light so as not to worry the children.

He didn't reply, but he did snap out of his motionlessness and rip the envelope open, yanking out a handwritten sheet. He unfolded it and started reading.

"Have you had enough, Javi?" I asked, as Javier swallowed his last bite. He was more prone to under-eating than either of the other two. He just nodded, and since I was pretty sure he'd managed almost two slices, I was happy.

"*I* want more!" said Polly, scowling at the empty toast racks. She had the opposite problem to Javier.

"*You've* had more than enough," I said firmly. "Anyway, you know *I want doesn't get*, so that's that."

Polly huffed. Roll on nine o'clock, when little Miss Grumpy would begin to turn into a bright and helpful little girl...

Luc was a fast eater, so despite all his time helping other people and fetching things, he'd not gone short of food. It was Bane who still had food on his plate, and me. In fact, Polly was eyeing her daddy's plate speculatively...

"Polly," I said under my breath, since Bane was absolutely fixated on the letter, "don't you even think about it."

But Bane lowered the letter—he'd finished reading—then brandished it at me. "What am I even supposed to... I don't even know... *Exactly what am I supposed to say to this?*"

He was frighteningly off balance. "What is it, love?"

He passed it across to me.

"Who's it from?" I asked.

"You don't recognize the writing?"

I glanced at it. "Not sure. Doesn't particularly ring a bell."

"Well, read it!"

I read 'To Mr. Verrall,' then...

"Mummy, can I leave the table?"

"Yes, of course, Luc. Would you look after Polly and Javi until it's time for school? Go and play in the other room." Since it looked like this mysterious letter was going to occupy me for a while.

"Of course, Mummy!" From the look Luc shot from Bane to me, he could tell something wasn't quite right, but fortunately looking after people and being given responsibility were two of his favorite things, so he held out a hand each to his brother and sister.

"Don't need looking after!" objected Polly.

"We'll both look after Javi, then. Come on, Javi..."

I turned my attention to the letter again.

To Mr. Verrall,

I have absolutely no desire to be writing this letter to you, but Mrs. Marsden insisted I do so or she would write herself. Since she should not be taxed in such a way, I have had to comply with her wishes. The fact is that Mrs. Marsden is suffering from metastasized cancer, still curable through organ transplantation at the time it was diagnosed, but just beyond the capabilities of those treatments still legal. In other words, thanks to the efforts of you and your unofficial registered partner, my wife is terminally ill.

I am writing because for reasons entirely incomprehensible to me, she wishes to see you. Since it is clearly impossible for you to come to the British department, she proposes to travel to Vatican State and visit you there. I am therefore writing to find out whether you are prepared to a) see her and if so, b) provide accommodation and medical care for the duration of her visit. I would of course be accompanying her.

I request that you respond promptly since she is really too frail to travel already and is certainly in no condition to undertake a wasted journey.

From,

Mr. Marsden

I looked up at Bane, who was still staring at the letter in my hands with a closed, frozen look, though a touch of bewilderment in his eyes told me that the news had struck him more deeply than he was perhaps willing to admit.

"What am I supposed to say to that?" he demanded again, when he saw me looking at him.

"Well... yes, and... yes?" I suggested.

Bane gripped the edge of the table with white knuckles, and glared at his toast as though it had done him a serious personal injury. Of course, it was not the toast that had done that.

"I thought," he said in a tight voice, "that I would never see them again. I was res... I was happy, to never see them again. Why would I want to?"

"Well, you can probably guess what I'm going to say."

"*She is my mother.* Never acted like it, though, did she?"

"Perhaps she's finally figured that out, and wants to mend things."

Bane snorted bleakly. "Yeah? More likely she wants to tell me one last time what a huge disappointment I was."

"You aren't seriously considering saying no, are you?"

Bane stared at the letter for several more long moments. When he finally spoke, his voice was heavy. "No. I suppose I can't say no, can I? However much I'd like to. Ugh!" He put his head in his hands and ran his fingers through his hair. "What do we tell the children? They'll be horrible to them!"

My heart also sank, at the thought of Bane's parents interacting with our children—and our friends. "We'll have to make it clear that they aren't their grandparents because they chose not to be. Surely then they won't expect too much." But even as I said it, my heart sank further. Whatever we said, the children would be wild with excitement at the thought of meeting their other grandparents. They'd scarcely encountered rudeness or true mean-spiritedness in their entire lives. Nothing we could say would prepare them.

"And what about Arthur and Almarda," said Bane. "They'd better not be mean to them!"

Almarda was tough as nails, but Arthur was a very sensitive child.

"I don't think they even know what 'Genetic Mix' means, yet," Bane added. "Polly and Javi certainly don't!"

"It's not such a big deal any more," I pointed out. "The Racial Breeding Laws are gone. Your parents always liked to follow the official line very closely, so maybe they won't say anything."

"Jane will probably slap them if they do," said Bane, a smile almost breaking through. "And they won't dare be rude to Bee, since he's the size of both of them put together!"

I mustered a laugh, at that. This could all be extremely unpleasant. But it was Bane's last chance to be reconciled with his mother, so it was terribly important, no matter how awful she'd been. Or perhaps precisely because of that.

"Do you think... your parents would come over? Bit of extra support for the children?" suggested Bane.

And for us... We could hardly ask Jon to come back, not in the middle of his big trip. "You write back to your... to Mr. Marsden." I checked my watch. "I'll give Mum a ring, I might just catch her."

15ᵗʰ September (26)

Only four days later Bane got another letter from Mr. Marsden, saying that they were setting off on the train the following evening and would arrive around midday the day after—which was the following day.

"Bother," said Bane, taking the letter back from me and reading it again. "That was quick. She must really be sick."

"I'm surprised Eliot isn't coming with her," I said.

"He must think she'll make it back," muttered Bane. "Unless he just isn't prepared to jeopardize his career, no matter what." Eliot Marsden had always been set on a career in the civil service. The EuroGov had made sure he got it, so that they could trot him out occasionally as an example of how a model citizen should behave.

"Still," murmured Bane, "I was hoping they might not get here quite this quickly..."

My mum and dad were arranging to come, but both had things they couldn't simply drop. They were going to arrive several days after the Marsdens, by the look of it, and who knew how long Bane's parents were actually planning to stay.

Bane was distracted all day, to put it mildly, and said almost nothing about the forthcoming visit. At bedtime he put on his pajamas, then just sat on the edge of the bed, staring into space, his shoulders rigid. The fact that he would be seeing his parents in less than twenty-four hours must be really sinking in by now.

When I was ready as well I climbed onto the bed behind him and tried to rub some of the tension out of his shoulders, but his muscles were too stiff. I slipped my arms around him instead. "Come one, Bane. Talk to me. It's like going to bed with an unexploded bomb."

He turned to me with an apologetic grimace. "Oh Margo, I'm sorry. It's just... well, I suppose I'm not talking because I'm not sure what I feel. Well, I feel so many things. I don't know where to start."

"Are you... *happy* that she wants to see you?"

"Well... provisionally, I suppose. I don't know what she wants, yet."

"What else do you feel?"

"Angry," said Bane, with a bit of a sigh. "And hurt. I've been trying so much to let it all go. I thought I was doing really well. Now it feels like it's all come right back. Boomerang rage."

I thought about my struggle to forgive Father Mark— and my still ongoing struggle to completely forgive Reginald Hill. "Yeah. Rage is like that."

"Also... hope," said Bane, speaking more freely now he'd started. "I suppose I do feel hope, but... not once in my life has hope ever been fulfilled, not by them. So I'm afraid to hope. I'd rather expect nothing from them, then they can't hurt me again."

After a moment he added, "Not that I've the foggiest what to expect. Which brings me back to that." He sighed.

"Well, I keep remembering what Father Mario said?" I told him. "About people seeing everything differently when they're dying?"

Bane nodded slightly. "Yeah, I keep thinking about that as well. He knew what he was talking about. He'd ministered to enough people in his time. Even if..." he broke off and laughed.

I knew what he was thinking. After Father Mario had delivered his wise words about how a terminal diagnosis caused people to re-evaluate all sorts of things in their life, Bane had promptly asked, "So do *you* see things differently?"

Father Mario had looked a little nonplussed, then admitted that actually, he didn't. "I think," he'd told us, "I've devoted my whole life to faith, and truth, and love, and those are the very things people regret not devoting enough time to. God knows there are plenty of times when I could have done better, but I don't look at my life and suddenly feel like I've made a huge mess of this or that, or, heaven forbid, all of it. Because some people do, I'm afraid."

Was Mrs. Marsden one of those people, by any chance? Surely she couldn't really be travelling all this way just to be mean to Bane one last time?

Bane gave another, almost unconscious sigh, then gave his head a slight shake as though to dismiss the whole matter. He turned around and slid an arm behind my back, his other hand caressing my belly, feeling for movement. "I'm sorry, little Helen-Francois, you probably think I've been ignoring you today. Daddy's still here. Are you going to say hello?"

16th September (26)

Shortly before midday Eduardo called to say that the Marsdens were on their way from *Roma Termini*. We duly trooped down to the Via di Belvedere to await their arrival, Luc clutching a bouquet of fuchsias he'd insisted on picking for his 'Other Grandmother' and Javi curled up in Bane's arms in an almost pre-lunch nap.

"You heard Daddy," Polly lectured her brothers, as we came within sight of St Anna's gate. "They don't like us! Giving them flowers won't help!"

Javi nestled his face more comfortably against Bane's chest, and closed his eyes a little further. Luc gave Polly something unusually close to a scowl. "We should show we're ready to like *them*," he said firmly. "Then if they're horrible, it won't be *our* fault."

"How did you get so wise?" I remarked, tousling his dark locks.

"Mummy!" He ducked away from me and pawed frantically at his hair. "I'm trying to look pre... presentable!"

"Did you get a secret paper craving and eat a dictionary while pregnant with him?" Bane asked, would-be lightly, but his tension was unmistakable.

"It would explain a lot, wouldn't it?" I quipped back.

"Why would it?" asked Luc. "The paper would just get di...gested, wouldn't it? And I don't think ink is good for you. I'm sure Grandma said it gives you.... what Other Grandma's got. You didn't eat a whole dictionary, did you, Mummy?"

"I didn't even eat a single page, Luc. Daddy was joking."

"Oh."

"He was *joking*," echoed Polly snidely. "You're being *stupid.*"

"So you got the joke, did you?"

"I'm not four yet," said Polly smugly. "*I'm* not stupid, just little."

I barely managed to keep from raising my hands to heaven. Luc's temper was very hard to find, but rather like Bane's when roused, so I scooped Polly up into my arms, prompting an outraged cry: "No! I'm not a baby!"

"You're only three and eleven months," I said firmly, "Very little. You just said it yourself. I'd better hold you for a while."

Polly huffed and fumed: she hated being babied. But before long she began to get awfully heavy, and when I saw Bane shooting me a look as though he was about to suggest we swap, I put her down. Javi was as close to a human stress-busting machine as anyone I'd ever met, whereas Polly... less so.

She promptly did a sort of triumphant war dance around Luc, who simply handed me his flowers for safe keeping and joined in. Javi opened his eyes and squirmed slightly, feeling left out, so Bane put him down so he could dance too. I smothered a sigh. But, looking at the children, I couldn't help a laugh.

"Hmm?" said Bane, his mind clearly far away.

I jerked my head to where Luc was dancing in circles, with his hands over his head, clapping and singing, "Alleluia' to his favorite tune, Polly was doing some sort of stomping, leaping dance that put me in mind of Africa, punctuated by a decidedly gung-ho chant of "Christ conquers, Christ reigns, Christ commands", and Javi was revolving unsteadily on the spot with his arms raised and his head tilted right up towards the blue sky above, humming a close approximation of my favorite *Te Deum* setting.

A smile succeeded in tugging at the corners of Bane's mouth. "Hello and welcome to the madhouse," he murmured.

But after a few more turns, Javi yawned and toddled back to Bane, arms held out, and Bane scooped him up again, Luc came to reclaim his flowers, and Polly started climbing into a nearby flowerbed.

"Don't you want to look presentable, too, Polly?" I asked her.

"Don't know what that means," she said, disappearing behind a bush.

"Your pants are smoking!" Luc called after her. "I told you yesterday!"

"Polly," said Bane, coming back to the present again, "Come out of there; they'll be here any minute."

"I'm 'sploring. I'm a 'splorer!"

"Well, I think you need to schedule your great expedition for another day," I put in. "Because a taxi has just pulled up at the gate."

Bane's head snapped around—he stared intently down Via di Belvedere to where St Anna's gate marked the boundary of Vatican Free State and EuroBloc. A Swiss Guard had just gone over to the taxi window and was checking who was who, whilst his comrade-in-arms remained in the bulletproof gate control booth, ready to lower the huge steel bollards to allow the car in or to call for backup, whichever was appropriate.

The taxi was the usual one the Vatican State employed to fetch guests from the station, and familiar enough to security, but the guard took something from the passengers—ID cards, no doubt—and slid them through the card slit into the booth. A few moments' wait, during which Polly came scrambling out of the bush and dropped down beside us, then a couple of Vatican passes came back through the slot. The Guard passed them into the taxi, argued with the occupants for a while, and finally waved the vehicle onwards.

As the taxi drove up the road towards us, I pulled a twig from Polly's hair and Javi peered at Bane and said, "Daddy?" in an anxious voice. Bane must be really tense.

"Everything's fine, Javi," Bane murmured, setting a kiss on our little boy's forehead. "Everything's fine." And a little tension did leave him. I could follow his chain of thought easily enough. Javi was safe and well in his arms, me and the other two also fine, so how bad was this visit really, compared to that?

The taxi was pulling up. The driver got out and hurried around to the boot, opened it and removed a couple of cases and a folding wheelchair, which he'd set up before the back door had even opened.

The years had not been particularly kind to Mr. Marsden—or perhaps it was just the last year—anyway, his hair was very grey and he'd put on a lot of weight. He didn't greet Bane; he didn't even look at him. He just concentrated on checking the wheelchair was up properly, then opening the other door and helping Mrs. Marsden out. Even with him providing a lot of support, she clung to the car as though in danger of crumpling.

Bane stepped forward uncertainly, but the taxi driver was already hovering. He leant in and lifted out a cylinder, transferring it to holder on the chair as Mr. Marsden got her settled into it. Oh, a piece of oxygen tubing was hooked under her nose, running to the cylinder. She really must be in a bad way.

When this was all done, the taxi driver smiled at everyone, closed the back door, got into the front seat and started the engine.

"Hey, don't you want paying?" said Mr. Marsden in Esperanto.

The taxi driver just waved a hand vaguely in the direction of St Peter's, towering nearby. "It is on the Vatican account; it is taken care of."

He drove off, leaving Mr. Marsden looking rather indignant.

"Well, you did ask for accommodation and everything," said Bane in English, clearly giving up on any proper greeting.

Mr. Marsden still didn't look at him. "I can't believe they took our ID cards!" he blustered to Mrs. Marsden. "How dare they!"

Mrs. Marsden didn't reply. She looked utterly exhausted. Her face was gaunt and shrunken, and she was wearing a woolly hat despite the mildness of the September day. Had she lost her hair?

"You'll get them back when you leave," said Bane levelly. "It's the same for everyone."

Mr. Marsden just looked down and fussed with the cases as though checking them.

Bane's temper was rarely ascendant these days, but right now I saw a spark of it flick through his eyes. "Look, Mr. Marsden," he said in a slightly harder voice, "I can promise you that I am under no illusions that *you* are here to see me. However, we are both adults and I think this will be much easier for everyone concerned if you are prepared to speak to me, at least about practical matters."

After another moment, Mr. Marsden raised his head, and finally looked at Bane. His gaze paused for a moment on the toddler Bane still held, but he simply gave a sharp nod.

Bane turned his attention to the woman in the wheelchair, and his tone softened a fraction. "Mrs. Marsden, I hope your journey hasn't been too tiring. Would you like to go straight to your room and rest?"

When he spoke, Mrs. Marsden raised her head to look at him properly. "Yes..." Her voice was very weak. But she went on, "Hello, Bane." Her eyes found me. "Hello, Margaret. It's been... a long time."

Mr. Marsden looked at me too, but harrumphed in disapproval. "We always thought you were such a good girl. Thought you'd be a good influence. It seems if anything it was the other way around! To think that he knew! That he *knew*, for all those years, what was going on at your house..."

"You make it sound like it was drug abuse or orgies or something," I couldn't help saying. "It was only Mass."

"Only!" spluttered Mr. Marsden. Clearly the whole religious freedom thing still hadn't quite sunk in for him.

"What's orgies?" asked Luc.

"What's drug abue?" asked Polly.

"Me and my big mouth," I muttered, as Bane raised an eyebrow and tried not to look amused. "I'll tell you when you're older." A lot older...

Mrs. Marsden was looking at the children now. Luc stepped forward determinedly, held out his posy and said very fast, in his best English, "We know you're not our grandma because you don't want to be but if you do want to be we'd like you to be, so these are for you..."

Mrs. Marsden blinked, as though following all that was a bit much for her tired mind, then seemed caught between pain and pleasure. "Oh... thank you... very kind..." she managed, accepting the flowers. For a moment it looked as though she would say something more, but she glanced at Mr. Marsden and fell silent.

She really looked like she was going to pass out if she didn't lie down soon. "Why don't we do proper introductions later," I said quickly, "when Mrs. Marsden has had a chance to rest."

"I should think so!" said Mr. Marsden, seizing the handles of the chair. "Which way?" Then he glanced at the cases. "Can that fellow bring those, since he's just standing around?" He nodded towards Snail, who hovered about a meter behind me.

Bane looked exasperated. "*That* is Margo's bodyguard, so no, he certainly cannot. Mrs. Marsden, would it tire you too much to have Javi on your lap, then I can bring the cases?"

"Why can't Margaret carry the kid?" snapped Mr. Marsden.

"She's pregnant and shouldn't be lugging things around," said Bane firmly.

"Pregnant?" said Mr. Marsden, in a tone of such horror you'd think it hadn't been all over the news two months ago. "But you've already *got* three children! That will make *four!*"

"So?" said Bane, settling Javi on Mrs. Marsden's lap. "Who says we'll stop at four, anyway? People are *not* having enough babies, y'know. Heard of population decline?"

Mr. Marsden looked scandalized, but Mrs. Marsden was too distracted by Javi to pay attention. Was Bane really going into protective overkill—hardly unlikely in the circumstances—or was he deliberately making his mother interact with our youngest, cutest, and most laid back child? Well, our youngest *born* child. I rubbed my stomach gently and led the way towards the Belvedere block.

It was late afternoon before the phone rang. It was Mr. Marsden calling to say that Mrs. Marsden was feeling somewhat rested and was hoping to see us again. I couldn't help doubting she could be all that recovered after such a long journey, but so little had been said before, the stress of not knowing what reception they were going to get was probably even worse.

I'd made sure to prepare enough food for two extra people, so Bane was able to simply invite them around for the evening meal. It sounded as though Mr. Marsden accepted the invitation with rather an ill grace.

"Well, you can go to the cafeteria on your own if you want," said Bane shortly. "I'm quite sure we're capable of giving Mrs. Marsden whatever assistance she needs. No? Well, in that case, dinner is the civilized thing, you know. Yes, I'll come and show you where to go." He rammed the receiver back down a bit harder than normal. "I wish he wasn't here," he said, through gritted teeth. "I wish he hadn't come. He's acting like an infant."

"Mrs. Marsden must have really wanted to see you or she wouldn't be here," I said. "Usually people want to see someone because they have something they want to say to them. She's not going to let him stop her, not after all this. Just don't expect her to necessarily spit it out immediately. If she has become aware of... of even *some* of her failings as your mother, that's not going to be an easy thing to admit to herself, let alone to you."

Bane rested a hand on my shoulder and dropped a kiss on my forehead in passing as he went to lay the table. "That's all very wise and true, Margo, but I really wasn't having some panic attack about him getting in the way of things. He just winds me up."

When Bane returned with the Marsdens, along with Luc and Polly, who'd been playing at Jane and U's, Mrs. Marsden still looked dreadfully tired, but she'd gone to the trouble of getting changed. Mr. Marsden was, probably pointedly, still wearing his travel-creased outfit.

"Well, now that we're all here," said Bane, lifting Javi out of the playpen, "let's make some introductions. Children, this is Mr. and Mrs. Marsden. Mr. and Mrs. Marsden, this is Lucas Mark Verrall, known as Luc, Dominique Polly Verrall, known as Polly, and Javier Luciano Verrall, known as Javi. In here," he placed a gentle hand on my belly, "is—probably—either Helen or François, we're not sure yet. You remember Margo, and I'm quite sure you remember me, seeing that we had the great mutual unhappiness of living in the same house for eighteen years."

Mrs. Marsden opened her mouth as though to say something, then closed it again. Then looked at the children and mustered a smile. "Nice to meet you properly. I've put those lovely flowers in water."

I'd have been more surprised at seeing the woman who'd treated Bane with cold dislike for his entire childhood being friendly to the children if it wasn't for the fact that she'd always been perfectly nice to me, and Kyle, and pretty much any child who wasn't her younger son.

Mr. Marsden looked at the children with disgust, though. "Some of those aren't British C names," he said indignantly.

"So?" said Bane.

Mr. Marsden scowled, but before he could say anything else, Mrs. Marsden lifted the shoebox she held on her lap and offered it to Bane. "I... brought your things," she said awkwardly.

Bane looked completely dumbfounded. "I assumed you'd burnt the lot!"

From the fact that Mr. Marsden was looking equally shocked, they had—or so he'd thought.

"Well, we... got rid of most of the stuff, of course." Mrs. Marsden had gone slightly pink and was avoiding both Bane's and Mr. Marsden's eyes. "But... well, it seemed a bit strange..." She stopped, then finished very quickly, "a bit strange to have a son for eighteen years and... and have absolutely nothing to show he ever existed. But... you should have this now."

Bane accepted the box from her, looking even more bemused. Had Mrs. Marsden never, despite what she said to the press at the time, been quite comfortable with the attempt to erase all memory of Bane from their lives?

Bane placed the box on the side table as though he would look at it later, but as he started to turn away, a look of sudden intentness, of hope, crossed his face. He swung around, yanked the lid off, and delved inside for a moment, then let out a joyful, "yes!" and held up a neatly sewn waterproof pouch.

I gasped. "Is it...?"

He was already slipping out a pretty little handmade book. He planted a kiss on it and immediately gathered me in his arms and kissed me too. "I can't believe it!" he whispered. *So happy about this!*

It had broken Bane's heart to leave the little book in Salperton, but he'd been practical enough to accept that it was too big to take on our hike across Europe. He'd scanned it and put the file on his phone, but always assumed that the original had been ceremonially burnt with everything else he'd left behind.

"Thank you," he told Mrs. Marsden, with obvious sincerity. "Thank you for saving this. It's..." he blushed slightly. "It's Margo's *proposal*, you see."

Mrs. Marsden went even pinker and looked at the carpet, as Mr. Marsden's face grew stormier, so it seemed a good moment to shepherd everyone to the table.

"Well, at least I don't have to worry about binding that new one anymore!" I said softly to Bane, as everyone got settled. He'd printed out a copy of the file several whole years ago, and I'd promised to bind it into a new book for him, but I'd been so busy... "I'll get rid of the print-out, shall I?"

"No, don't do that. You can keep it."

"It's *your* story..."

"So I can give you a copy if I want, can't I?"

I conceded with a smile. Instead of binding the print-out into a book, I could bind it into the back of this diary instead. That would be nice. *I've been dying to annotate it!*

Everyone was settled; it was time to eat. I'd made a simple British roast and even Mr. Marsden tucked in with grudging enthusiasm. *Now I can!*

Mrs. Marsden seemed to have little appetite, though, and after struggling through a slice of meat, two potatoes and a small spoonful of peas, she put down her knife and fork. After a few minutes recovering from the effort of eating, she said in her thin voice, "So... what have you been doing with yourself, Bane?" The awkward and rather unnecessary question was clearly meant as an icebreaker.

Bane put down his own fork and cleared his throat slightly. "Well, I'm a father now, obviously. Four times over. I look after the children quite a lot, because Margo's so busy, though childcare isn't something one has to worry about, living here. Fighting off the eager helpers is more the issue.

"And, uh, as you probably know, the main thing I do is to facilitate people's emigration from the EuroBloc, especially if they need to leave quickly for some good reason, such as a fourth child on the way. Used to be the third child, of course. I... can't really go into details about that, other than what goes on the mission blog. It's classified, you know."

He seemed to grope for something that would actually be new information, and waved towards the rows of pots on the window ledges. "Oh, I, uh, look after our plants as well."

Mrs. Marsden looked astonished. "*You* do?"

Bane nodded and shrugged, "Yeah, well, they're terribly important to Margo, but with the best will in the entire world, she's not really capable of keeping them alive, so I took over. I'm doing a little better."

"A *lot* better," I put in dryly. "We've only lost one since then."

"Well I never," was all Mrs. Marsden said to that. But... picturing an angry Bane, age nine, hacking down every plant in her garden?

Bane frowned slightly. Was *he* remembering being shut in his room for a week with nothing but bread and water in punishment for that misdeed? His father had stopped beating him for his misbehavior by then, because Bane had got large enough to hit back with a little more force than Mr. Marsden cared to be on the receiving end of. I'd come round every day and tied a bundle of food to the string Bane let down from his window, so he hadn't actually gone hungry after the first day or two, but it was clear the memory still hurt.

Of course, Bane shouldn't have ruined the garden, but... why *had* Bane launched that attack on his mother's flowerbeds? Was that the time she'd screamed that she wished infanticide was permitted on healthy newborns because she'd have disposed of him the moment he was born? Hard to keep track of all the hurtful things she'd said, but no, it wasn't that... Ah yes, that was it. The destruction of the garden had been triggered by the first—though not the last—time she'd yelled at him that she wished she'd had an abortion and would have done if she'd known what he was going to be like...

Bane was now shooting Mrs. Marsden a look of mingled pain and wariness that made it clear he was again doubting whether she really meant him well.

"Well, times change," said Mrs. Marsden. Not missing Bane's expression? "People... change. Look at you, you're all grown up, now. Very brave. Helping people..."

Mr. Marsden gave an enormous snort. "Helping people violate the law? Helping them put themselves in a position whereby they'll never be able to return to the EuroBloc? You call that *helping?*"

"They don't *want* to go back," said Bane, in a rather patient voice. "They think their child is more important than whatever they're leaving behind; more important than anything." His voice became edged. "*Some* parents do take that attitude."

Maybe it was wishful thinking, but I wasn't sure Mrs. Marsden didn't flinch slightly, at that.

Perhaps fortunately, at this point Polly, who'd been preternaturally good due to a combination of the strangers and her interest in her dinner, piped up with, "Why are you wearing a plastic tube on your face, not-Grandma?"

"*Polly,*" I said.

"Oh, no, it's okay. Uh..." Mrs. Marsden touched the tube with a frail hand. "Well, it gives me extra oxygen, Polly. Makes me feel better."

"What's wrong with you?"

"Well, I've... I've got... well, I'm very sick."

"Are you going to heaven soon?"

"*Polly!*" I hissed.

"Oh good grief!" said Mr. Marsden. "You haven't allowed them to be stuffed full of superstitious nonsense, have you?" That seemed to be directed at Bane, who didn't dignify it with a reply.

"What's 'su-su-stish nonsense'?" asked Polly.

"Mr. Marsden's ideas, that's what," said Bane, not quite under his breath.

"So, are you?" Luc asked Mrs. Marsden.

"Am I what?"

"Going to heaven soon?"

"Luc!" I said.

"What? What did we do?"

"People... people don't like to talk about it, you know!"

"Yes, they do. Uncle Mario was always talking about it! And Sister Umgerda. And..."

"Yes, but... not *everyone* does."

"Why not?" chorused Luc and Polly together.

"They just *don't*," I said very firmly, since Mrs. Marsden was looking extremely distressed by the turn of the conversation and the fact she'd been unable to bring herself to speak the word 'cancer' rather suggested she was not someone who was up for talking about her imminent departure from this life.

Lord? It would be wonderful if we could change that...

20th September (26)

The next couple of days were a bit anti-climactic. Though she tired quickly, Mrs. Marsden seemed keen to spend time with us, perhaps especially with the children, but showed no inclination to discuss anything weighty or serious. Her interactions with Bane were polite but awkward, which was a huge improvement, but explained nothing. Could she have changed at all, even before the terminal diagnosis? It had actually been almost a decade since Bane—since either of us—had seen her. Was she here for reconciliation? The mere fact of her presence seemed to imply it, yet... she said nothing.

"What does she *want?*" Bane would mutter to himself; it was obviously getting to him.

On Thursday morning, Luc dressed at breakneck speed and tumbled into the living room only minutes after I'd woken him.

"Can I go ahead to Mass, Mummy?"

"Uh, yes, of course, Luc." He was almost old enough to have the run of the State, now. "You're not up to something, are you?"

His eyes opened wide and earnest. "No, Mummy! Other-Granny wanted to know why we're always up so early, so I told her to be ready at seven-fifteen..." he shot a look at the clock on the wall.

I stared at him. "*Mrs. Marsden* wants to come to Mass?"

"Oh, she doesn't know it's Mass! I said it would be a surprise!"

"Riiiiight... well, go ahead, just... don't be too hurt if she doesn't take it very well."

Luc nodded, grinned, and was off through the door.

"There goes a natural born optimist," said Bane, from Polly's room. He'd clearly heard. "I hope she isn't too awful about it."

Bane had clearly spent the last few days, nerves screwed up tight, waiting for his mother to do something horrible.

"I hope not too," I replied, "but it might be the only way to get her there, so better not to interfere, right?"

"Umm."

Although Mr. Marsden tended to greet their every mention of faith with mutters about brainwashing, it had already occurred to me that simply leaving Mrs. Marsden with the children might be the best way to facilitate her conversion. Our Vatican-raised children chattered about faith just as freely and naturally as they talked about the football league or what film was showing at the State's little cinema this week. No one interacting with them could avoid being dunked into a worldview saturated by God's presence.

When Bane and I arrived in St Peter's with Polly and Javi, we found Mrs. Marsden in her wheelchair, parked at the end of our usual pew. Luc sat beside her, head close to hers, pointing this way and that as he whispered to her about his favorite statue and favorite inscription and favorite whatever.

Mr. Marsden—my heart leapt slightly—wasn't anywhere in sight. Mr. Marsden had been sticking to his registered partner like a bur, and somehow I couldn't help feeling that getting Mrs. Marsden on her own, even for the length of Mass, was a positive development.

Mrs. Marsden had a look of mingled panic and dismay on her face, and seemed to be listening to Luc with a certain amount of effort. "I'm really not sure..." she put in, when he paused to draw breath.

"No, you'll enjoy it, really." Luc put his missal into her lap and opened it up. "Look, you can borrow this, I know the words. You can just read along if you like. You don't have to part... participate."

"I..." said Mrs. Marsden weakly, "I... Philip wouldn't like..."

"So?" said Luc, sounding for a moment rather like his Daddy. "He doesn't own you. You can do what you want. Won't you stay? It'll be great!"

Perhaps his beseeching look did the trick, or perhaps Mrs. Marsden was secretly curious, either way, she was still there when Mass started, and Luc busied himself helping her keep her place, throughout.

"How was it?" he asked, as he pushed her chair back towards our block afterwards.

"Well... odd. It was all rather odd."

"Ah, yes," said Luc wisely, nodding to himself. "I suppose because you are—what did Daddy call it?—um, religiously illit...erate, that's it, you wouldn't understand everything very well."

Mrs. Marsden shot Bane a look somewhat more like her old self, but Luc was burbling on like a cheerful stream, "But never mind the words, how *was* it?"

For a moment I thought Mrs. Marsden would claim not to know what he meant, but eventually she just said, "Peaceful, I suppose."

"See! I said you'd like it! Will you come tomorrow?"

"Well, I don't know..."

"Oh, go on, say you will!"

"Well, *maybe*..."

"Yes..."

I'd half expected Mr. Marsden to be lying in wait for us, but there was still no sign of him. Bane must've noticed the same thing, because he said, "Would you like to come to our place for a spot of breakfast, Mrs. Marsden?"

"Oh, ah..."

"Luc's taking Polly and Javi to the cafeteria for breakfast this morning," I put in.

Luc shot me a disappointed look that said, "I am?" clearly enough, but kept his mouth shut.

Mrs. Marsden still looked uncertain, almost fearful. Did she actually want to get Bane completely on his own? Or was that precisely what she was afraid of? "I might join them," I suggested.

"No," said Bane sharply. "You've... you've got that... thing... this morning... Remember?"

Bane was not willing to be completely alone with *her.* Well, that was her fault for how she'd treated him in the past. "Oh, yes. Of course. That thing..." Providing Bane with moral support... "Won't you join us, Mrs. Marsden?"

"Well..." She seemed to be gathering her courage. "Yes, I will. Thank you."

I'd had enough experience with Mrs. Marsden's lack of appetite by now that I didn't offer a cooked breakfast, and Bane and I quickly brought out cereal and toast. I also quietly took both phones off the hook. Buy us a bit of time if Mr. Marsden started searching for his Registered Partner. Though no doubt he thought Mrs. Marsden was off on some harmless excursion with her grandson. He'd shown no interest in getting to know the children himself.

"So, uh, how's Eliot?" I asked, once we all had some food in front of us, seeking some as-yet-untapped topic to get the conversation started.

Mrs. Marsden seemed glad of a chance to stop spooning cereal. "Oh, he's very well. Recently received promotion at work; you may have seen it on the news if you still keep an eye on the local papers. He's head of Flood Protection for the whole of the Salperton area now. And I'm sure you know he Registered three years ago; that was in the Department-wide press. A lovely girl, British C, *of course...*"

Mrs. Marsden had met Jane and U's children, and been civil to them, but clearly realized that her last comment had strayed onto controversial ground. "Anyway," she hurried on, "they had a lovely Registration party. The Mayor attended. They get on rather well, you see." Her pride in her eldest son was obvious, and I wished I hadn't brought him up.

Bane's shoulders were tense, and I'd a feeling it was pain not anger. Or not just anger. But he made an effort to speak naturally. "And how's it going in the family way? A little girl? A little boy? I suppose they might even have two by now."

Mrs. Marsden lowered the spoon she had just raised to her lips with a shaking hand, and placed it back in the bowl. "No children yet, actually," she said in a very collected voice. "But we confidently expect news... very soon."

Eliot Marsden had no children yet? He'd not registered until twenty-five, which would have counted as rather late whilst the Stable Population Act was still in force—though the EuroGov had been flaunting his unRegistered self as evidence that *of course people didn't feel pressurized to secure an acceptable partner and register as early as possible.*

But he was now twenty-eight and had only two years until the time when, previously, the Stable Population Board would legally have had the right to force him and his partner to unRegister and reRegister with someone else.

It was something they'd rarely enforced, and then only when they had strong suspicions a couple weren't actually trying, but all the same. Under the old laws, certainly amongst EGD supporters like the Marsdens, there was a considerable stigma attached to arriving at the age of thirty childless. Eliot was cutting it close. And if three years of trying hadn't produced a child, there was an increasing possibility that something was actually wrong.

No wonder Mrs. Marsden was so interested in our children. Oh dear, might that be the only reason she'd come? They were, after all, the only grandchildren she'd had any hope of meeting.

From the crease in Bane's brow, this unpleasant possibility had also occurred to him. And clearly he'd had enough of all this uncertainty, because he said, firm but polite, "Mrs. Marsden, would you mind me asking why you have come here? Was it to see me, or the children? If it's the latter, just say so. We're not going to throw you out for wanting to know your grandkids. You *do* consider them to be your grandchildren, don't you?"

Mrs. Marsden licked her cracked lips, looking taken aback by this plain talking. It was a moment before she replied, very quietly. "Yes... Yes, they're my grandchildren. Do you want me to... I'm not sure how to do the paperwork, from here..."

"I don't care what some piece of paper back in London says," said Bane. "I only care whether you acknowledge them. And whether you acknowledge me. Not that I'm quite sure how you'd separate the two, but I'm hardly going to take anything for granted when it comes to you."

Mrs. Marsden gave another of her almost imperceptible winces. "I... I did come to see *you*, Bane. The children... the children are just so delightful. Even..." She seemed to struggle with herself for a moment, then managed, "Even your friends' children. Little Arthur and... I can't pronounce her name. But she's lovely."

From someone who'd spent her life parroting the EGD's bile about Genetic Mixes, this was quite a concession.

"And... *why* did you want to see me?" asked Bane. He was pushing, but waiting for Mrs. Marsden to raise such issues was beginning to seem a lost cause, especially when Mr. Marsden was at her shoulder. And she hadn't really got any stronger since she arrived, even once she'd had time to rest properly after the journey. Rather the opposite. Doctor Frederick couldn't tell us anything about her condition, of course, because of confidentiality, but I'd a feeling we—or rather she—didn't have a lot of time.

"I..." Mrs. Marsden swallowed with difficulty, and adjusted her oxygen tube. A sheen of sweat covered her brow. This whole conversation was clearly as stressful for her as for Bane. "Well, I... It's just... whatever that thing we signed says... well, you *are* actually my son, biologically. It just... well, it didn't seem, it didn't seem right that things should... should be like this between us."

"All right," said Bane, his voice still very controlled. "Well, to be quite honest, I haven't changed that much. I keep my temper better, I'm a bit more patient, a bit less reckless. But I still think the EGD are evil and the EuroGov *aren't* a democracy. In fact, I now don't just think that people shouldn't be killed for believing in God, I believe in God too. So from that point of view I imagine you think I've got worse. Now, tell me that you don't believe I would ever have responded to a kind word or a scrap of appreciation and I'll call you a liar. Which means I haven't changed. So I think the ball is squarely in your court on this one."

Mrs. Marsden fidgeted with her oxygen tube again, her head turning away slightly, as though seeking escape from Bane's words. "Oh, why do you always have to be so *difficult?"* she said fretfully.

"Difficult?" echoed Bane, and I could tell he was beginning to struggle to hold onto his hard-learnt control. "Are you saying you think everything that is wrong between us is because I'm *difficult?* That it's all *my* fault?"

Mrs. Marsden twisted her frail hands together. "I... I don't know, Bane. You... you were *so* difficult. So *angry.* Always out to spite us. Thwart us. Make our lives miserable. Anything you could think of..."

"Why was I angry, Mother?" Bane bit the words off as though trying to bite back a life-time's pain-fueled rage.

"I don't know," said Mrs. Marsden plaintively. "I never *knew...*"

Bane's chest was heaving and his hands were clenching together now. "Answer me this, Mother," he said tightly. "Was I a difficult baby?"

Mrs. Marsden looked slightly relieved, clearly feeling this supported her case. "Oh, *yes.* Very difficult. Always screaming and crying."

"Really? Margo's mother once described me as a well-behaved baby. Sweet and affectionate, are the words she used. And did she ever complain of bad behavior when I was around at their house? So, why do you think I was so different when I was with her?"

Mrs. Marsden was silent. So silent it was deafening. Her face actually whitened a little.

"Shall I tell you why?" Bane was almost snarling. "Because she treated me the same as she treated Margo and Kyle. Because she looked at me and saw something precious and valuable. *Because she loved me!"*

Mrs. Marsden had put a hand to her heaving chest. "Bane," she said faintly, "Bane, you don't understand how difficult it was for me... Back then, you know how it was back then. It was so difficult. I felt so *ashamed.* So humi-liated. Anyone who saw you would have *assumed.* Assumed you were a Genetic Mix. Every time I went out in public with you, the shame ate into me. Every time I even *looked* at you...

"And it was so *unfair.* So unfair. We hadn't done anything wrong! If only you'd looked like Eliot! If only you'd been ugly or... or fat... or... anything else! Can't you understand how awful it was, to be your mother?"

Bane stood up so fast his chair flew backwards into the wall.

"NO!" he roared. "NO, I CAN'T! I never could, and now I'M a father, I understand it even less! If one of my children did something really awful—I don't know, became a rabid atheist and went off and lived in sin, or... or murdered someone or something like that—I would STILL LOVE THEM! Just as much as ever! And that's something they might CHOOSE to do! I didn't CHOOSE to be born looking this way! But you punished me for it every day of my life! And YOU dare to whine about UNFAIRNESS!"

Tears were running down his cheeks now. "I was your *CHILD.* It shouldn't have mattered to you what I *did,* let alone what I LOOKED LIKE! You should have loved me all the same. A parent's love should be UNCONDITIONAL, how can you not understand that? How can you act baffled about what was wrong between us! YOU NEVER LOVED ME! That's what was wrong! YOU! NEVER! LOVED! ME! And until you can accept that, there's no point me talking to you!"

He marched around the side of the table furthest from Mrs. Marsden, straight to the door, and reached out a hand to open it.

"B... Bane..." quavered Mrs. Marsden.

Bane stopped with his hand on the latch, but didn't turn around. He wanted to leave, I could tell. He wanted to get out of there. And preferably smash something. He'd not done that for years.

"Bane... pl...please don't leave."

Bane turned around and put his back to the door, not going any closer to her.

"I... uh... I..." Mrs. Marsden seemed to be struggling for words. Tears were starting to track down her cheeks, and finally her face crumpled and she began to sob. She managed to get a few words out, in-between gasps. "Don't... go... Right... you're right... terrible mother... Making excuses... no excuse... I'm sorry... I'm sorry... I'm sorry..."

After a few moments of this, Bane finally uncoiled from against the door and slowly approached her. He sat gingerly in the neighboring chair and after some hesitation, took her hand in his. She cried even harder, clutching his hand in both of her own.

It perhaps didn't seem like much, but it was probably the first affectionate touch they'd ever exchanged.

After a while Bane supplied his mother with a hankie and actually rested a hand on her shoulder in awkward comfort. She smiled and sniffed and kept tight hold of his other hand.

Thank you, Lord. I couldn't help feeling that Mrs. Marsden had come along with little more than a vague hope that in some miraculous, Hollywoodesque way, everything would resolve itself without her actually having to face up to her failings as a mother. Like that would have happened. Good thing Bane had pushed so hard.

"Are you all right?" Bane was asking her softly, now there seemed slightly more chance of her being able to answer. "Do you need a rest? I... I am really sorry you're... sick, you know."

She blew her nose again, patting his hand with her other one. "Can't be helped," she whispered. "Can't be helped."

This astonishingly cordial exchange was disturbed by a sharp knock at the door. My heart sank slightly. When I answered it, it was indeed Mr. Marsden.

"Is Portia here? I've just seen those children running wild in the garden; if they've *left* her somewhere... Ah, Portia, good." His eyes narrowed as he took in the cozy scene, and he seemed to be reconsidering his last word. "What's going on?"

"We've been having a spot of breakfast," I said. Mrs. Marsden, to her credit, had not let go of Bane's hand. "Have you eaten? Would you care to join us?"

"I've had something," said Mr. Marsden brusquely, eyes still on Mrs. Marsden. He moved forward purposefully. "Portia, let's go and take a walk outside. We must be getting back to Eliot soon, and we haven't seen all the historic architecture yet."

"Ah. No, Philip," said Mrs. Marsden, holding up a restraining hand as he reached for the handles of her chair. "I'm going to stay and talk to Bane some more, then have a rest. And..." she took a deep breath, "and I don't want to go back. Maybe Eliot could join us here."

"*Here?* Preposterous! What about his career? Did you think of that? What would it look like if he visited the *Vatican Free State!*"

"Well, he doesn't have to come," said Mrs. Marsden querulously, adjusting her oxygen tube and breathing deeply through her nose, then adding more softly, "But I hope he does."

"How can you do this to your own son? You told him you'd be back!"

"Plans change. Anyway, I really can't face the journey." And she looked so tired it was clear that this wasn't wholly an excuse.

"You'd rather ask *this* of him? For *what!*"

"I want to spend the time with Bane and our grand-children." Mrs. Marsden's voice was getting sharp. "Eliot's had my attention for twenty-eight years, he can hardly complain." Her voice softened again. "But... please persuade him to come, won't you, Philip?"

Mr. Marsden was starting to look plain furious. He jabbed a finger at Bane, and came close to yelling. "It's *his* fault they can't cure you, him and that superstitious fanatic he calls wife! *His* fault, do you understand? He might as well have killed you with his own two hands! And now you'll spurn the only son you legally have, for him? For your... your *murderer!*"

Bane was starting to scowl, but I detected anxiety in the set of his shoulders. Afraid Mr. Marsden was about to torpedo his new-found relationship with his mother?

Mrs. Marsden was silent for a few moments. Utterly exhausted by all this? Or thinking... because eventually she spoke in a very collected way. "Philip, you remember that period shortly before the vote, when I was out of work?"

Mr. Marsden looked baffled. "Of course."

"And you remember our neighbors at the time? The young couple with the preKnown."

"Of course. What...?"

"Well, at the time I was out of work, they were really struggling. Harry had been made redundant, and had to take a rather worse paid job, so Tilda needed to go out to work until they found a cheaper place to live. But they couldn't afford the childcare, and the school wouldn't let Kelly attend, so they were in a fix."

"So...?"

"So, I hadn't found work yet, and was at home all day, and I figured even if they paid me less than a nursery, I'd be earning something. So I agreed to look after the... after Kelly, while her mum was out at work."

Mr. Marsden looked aghast. "You were looking after a *preKnown*? *That* was your 'little bit of work from home'?"

"Yes," said Mrs. Marsden, very composedly. "I knew how you'd react, so I didn't mention it. We needed the income and Tilda needed the help. I figured I could put the preKnown in a play pen most of the time and get on with the housework. As long as she had her lunch, and her nappy changed when needed, there'd be no need to trouble myself with her. She was extremely subnormal, after all."

Bane's nostrils flared and his shoulders went very tense. I could almost taste his sudden anger. That was exactly the way she'd treated him as a young child, on those days when my mum couldn't look after him. In the pen and ignored all day, like some unwanted pet. Mrs. Marsden was too intent on Mr. Marsden to notice his reaction.

"You didn't think about what the other neighbors would think?" Mr. Marsden seemed to be close to writhing in retroactive social embarrassment.

"They clearly thought it a very sensible arrangement, since they obviously all took care not to mention it to you." Mrs. Marsden spoke rather dryly.

"But... but what is your point? Why are you telling me this *now?*"

"Because Kelly wasn't quite what I expected. Oh, she was stupid, in an intellectual way. Eight years old and couldn't talk very well at all, didn't understand what colors were, what numbers were, didn't get anything like that. But she had a... a joy... a... a life, to her, that was really quite... quite lovely. And... a good nature. Such a good nature. She always wanted to help.

"Increasingly I'd get her out of the pen and she'd trail around the house, 'helping' with the housework. I mostly gave her made-up jobs, of course, like you do with a small child, but all the same, she was... she was such a joy to have around. When they found a new place and moved, around the same time I got a new job, well, quite frankly I really missed her."

Mr. Marsden looked caught between horror and disgust. "And?" he said warily.

"And when the Vote came along, only three months later, I couldn't get Kelly out of my head. Oh, I knew all the rational arguments for Sorting backwards and forwards, and I believed them, or thought I did..."

I was beginning to get an inkling of what might be coming, and from Mr. Marsden's expression, he was too, though he wasn't going to believe it until he actually heard it.

"An adult preKnown is nothing but a burden on society!" said Mr. Marsden heatedly. "What use could that Kelly girl have possibly been to anyone? The only thing she could do for society was to provide healthy organs to cure more productive members. And thanks to *them*," he jerked his head at Bane and me, "that's not going to happen. All of us will simply be paying for her useless carcass for the rest of her natural life!

He went on savagely, "A couple of organs from someone like her and you'd be living a normal span, a hundred, a hundred and ten, maybe more. You'd be looking forward to seeing Eliot's children, and your great-grandchildren. Instead of making do with *his* deranged mutts." He jerked his head at Bane again. "A child like Kelly would have saved your life!"

Mrs. Marsden nodded. "So goes the rational argument, and I intended to hold to it, however often I thought of Kelly. But when I got in the voting booth, I couldn't escape one simple fact. If I tapped the 'yes' box, to continue Sorting, I was signing Kelly's death warrant. And however clear it might be, in pure reason, that my life was worth more than hers, I could not bring myself—all hypothetical back then, of course—but I could not bring myself to buy my life with hers."

She shook her head to herself. "That bright, happy, innocent little girl. Taken away, just like Margaret. And what a shock *that* was. I know you felt that, Philip; I know you did. I cried all evening, and I saw you wiping your eyes a time or two."

"Margaret was a useful member of society!" said Mr. Marsden with an air of desperation. "It was obvious they'd put the bar in the wrong place when it came to her! Of course, I didn't know about her superstitious leanings, then..."

"Maybe. But when it came down to it, it wasn't about whether Kelly was useful. Though, thinking about it since, I've concluded that her happiness is very useful. Quite an under-rated contribution, in a way. But anyway, I meant to tick 'yes', but I couldn't do it. Eventually I tapped 'no' and I hit the button to register my vote, and it was done. So my current predicament is my fault as much as it is Bane's fault, or Margaret's fault, or anyone else's fault. I voted to end Sorting."

"No..." whispered Mr. Marsden, staring at her as though she'd transformed into someone else right in front of his eyes.

"I'm sorry," Mrs. Marsden said quietly. "I didn't tell you because I didn't want to upset you, and because to begin with, I wasn't sure I'd done the right thing. Some days I regretted it a lot. But, gradually... I became satisfied I'd done a good thing, that the rational arguments just weren't... watertight. Weren't... enough.

"I got in touch with Kelly again, once I knew she would live. She's sixteen now. Out of nappies years ago. She's working in the same shop as her mother. She stacks the shelves and fetches and carries, and smiles at all the customers, and packs their bags for them. But... I've concluded it wouldn't matter even if she hadn't become such a productive member of society. It simply wouldn't have been *right* to kill her."

"Really?" snapped Mr. Marsden. "Even *now?* You still think that?"

"I am... trying to be... thankful... that when the vote happened I was in good health," said Mrs. Marsden honestly. "It is... more than likely... that I might otherwise have been tempted into making a serious mistake."

"Mistake? *Mistake?*" spluttered Mr. Marsden. He pointed at me. "You... you sound like you've swallowed one her books!"

"You should read one. She makes a good case for Sorting not being nearly so rational as we were taught to believe."

"Gah!" Mr. Marsden literally threw up his hands and stormed out of the apartment, slamming the door with an enormous thud.

I let out a long breath, and could see Bane doing the same. Although Mrs. Marsden still seemed to have lingering prejudice against Genetic Mixes, it was clear that in the last decade her ideas on Sorting had undergone a quiet revolution, so quiet even her Registered Partner hadn't known. Had that also influenced her decision to come here?

But Mrs. Marsden was breathing too fast; she clutched her tube to her nose and leant over, her elbows on the table.

Bane put a hand on her shoulder again. "Hey, it's okay, calm down. He'll cool off, you know he will."

"Yes... yes, I know. I'm... I'm so *tired...*"

"I'm quite sure you need to rest, after all that. Look, why don't you just have a lie down here for a while?"

"Yes... yes, I need to lie down..."

Bane settled his mother on our bed for a nap, and she stayed there all morning. Mr. Marsden was nowhere to be found when we tried to issue a lunch invitation, but a quick call to Eduardo calmed Mrs. Marsden's fears that he'd left: he was at the top of St Peter's dome, ostensibly taking photographs, but really sulking. Or possibly recovering enough puff to walk down those five hundred and fifty-one steps again.

Mrs. Marsden spent a quiet afternoon talking—somewhat stiltedly—with Bane. By the evening, Mr. Marsden was back in their room, and when I issued a dinner invitation, he snarled that he would come. It was clear he was mightily upset, but that Mrs. Marsden's condition made him reluctant to hold a grudge. Whatever their grievous faults, there'd never been any doubt that Mr. and Mrs. Marsden did genuinely love each other.

Half way through the meal, there was a knock on the door. I went to look through the peep hole, and swung the door open eagerly.

"Granny! Grandpa!" The children leapt from their chairs and hurtled towards us like three metal balls towards a pair of magnets.

I had to wait for my hug from Mum and Dad. "Come and sit down. Do you want something to eat? I'm sure I can find something."

Bane came to get a hug as well, as Mum said, "We ate on the ship. And a stupid idea that was; I felt sick all the way to Rome. But didn't you know we were arriving?"

Eduardo hadn't let us know. He probably didn't feel the Marsdens were to be trusted with information about when my parents were crossing EuroBloc territory. "Well, come and sit down," I said again. "Bane's mum and Mr. Marsden are here already, as you can see."

"Portia!" said Mum, advancing with a big smile. "Philip! How good to see you!"

Neither of them smiled back. Mrs. Marsden looked decidedly grim. "I don't see what advantage it is for you to pretend you like us *now*," she said cuttingly.

"You used us!" said Mr. Marsden, more angrily. "Shamelessly! Used us to cover up your seditious activities!"

"Ah, right," said Mum, "we'd better clear this up straight away. Yes, we chose to pursue a friendship with you in the beginning, for, shall we say, tactical, reasons. No, the friendship itself wasn't false. We genuinely considered you to be our friends, we still do, and we are pleased to see you again. Although I am very sorry for your present ill health, Portia."

"We're very sorry for any embarrassment our departure caused you, as well," said Dad quietly. "It simply couldn't be helped in the circumstances. As for the rest, we would apologize for not telling you, but I think you were much happier not knowing."

"And I'm sure you'll agree it was a lot safer for us," said Mum dryly.

Mrs. Marsden looked slightly uncomfortable, and finally gave Mum a stiff smile. I don't think any adult in the room doubted that the Marsdens would have turned my parents in, if they'd found out they were in the Underground.

"What was safer?" asked Luc.

"Nothing. Come and sit down again, children. Bane, can you find a couple of extra chairs?"

Bane had to get Dad to help him carry in a couple of huge antiques from the main corridor, but soon we had enough seats.

"Granny, did you bring us anything from Africa?" asked Polly.

"I did, actually," smiled Mum. "But I'm not sure where it's got to..."

"Is it a hamster?" shrieked Polly.

"Better than that," smiled Mum, just as there was another knock on the door. "Ah, there we are."

I went for the door again, and Bane followed, since he hadn't sat down yet. Outside stood a familiar figure...

"Uncle Jon!" came three shrieks from behind us, and the floor shivered under the incoming stampede...

"Jon!" I gasped, as he tousled heads and hugged a child with each arm. "What are you doing here?"

"Well, I thought I would bundle together all my days off for the trip and pop back for a visit," he said, with a shrug that tried to imply it was no big deal.

When Bane stepped forward and hugged him, slightly harder and longer than usual, words of appreciation were rendered unnecessary.

I was so glad to see him. You know, even after all this time, things never seem quite so bad if all 3 of us are around. I know what you mean.

4th October (26)

Mrs. Marsden grew frailer and frailer. She spent almost all her time with either Bane or the children, but she had to spend more and more of the day resting. She started allowing Luc to take her to Mass every morning, though, which I could tell made Bane very happy. Gradually she grew a little more relaxed when it came to speaking about her impending death, and eventually she divulged that when she'd left home, she'd been told she only had about a fortnight left. Since she had now exceeded that, even Mr. Marsden began to grudgingly admit that the trip had been good for her in some ways.

It was clear enough, though, that in a matter of days, now, she would be bedbound. Luc wheeled her off to see his Godfather, Pope Cornelius, a couple of times, and now and then I heard him earnestly lecturing her: "You do need to make your mind up, you know." Bane and I took care not to press her on religious matters, deeming any approach from us likely to be highly counter-productive, but surprisingly, she showed an interest in speaking to Jon privately.

Mr. Marsden looked on in quiet horror, with the air of a man who feels everything is slipping through his fingers. What he said in private, who knew, but she continued to allow Luc to catechize her in his simple, childish—but accurate enough—way.

Eliot was still resisting, certain that if he just waited long enough, his mother would come back. A notion he was only eventually disabused of when his father snatched the phone from his sobbing mother and yelled that, "She's not bloody coming back, so get your ass over here before it's too late!" which was more bad language than I'd heard from him in my entire life.

So Eliot came. I cooked a nice dinner and worried that this might be even more unpleasant than the arrival of the Marsdens senior. The children were duly warned that their Not-Uncle Eliot was Not-Nice compared to their Uncle Kyle, or any of their legion of honory uncles.

"He can hang out with not-Grandfather, then," was Luc's response. Mr. Marsden remained stand-offish with them.

A VSS agent brought Eliot up to our apartment when he arrived, since Mrs. Marsden was in no condition to go down to meet him. As soon as the VSS guy had gone, Eliot Marsden raked the assembled group—Bane and myself, the children, Mum and Dad, and Jon—with a look that combined cold disdain and cold fury, announced, "I do not even wish to speak to any of you," and marched forward to give his mother a decidedly angry hug.

"Don't you understand!" he hissed at her. "Don't you understand what this could do to my career? Don't you care?"

"You sound just like your father," said Bane, "And I think seeing that our mother spent most of the day resting so she could be here tonight, you might try being a bit nicer to her."

"You seem to have covered yourself well enough, anyway," I added dryly. Earlier Eduardo had directed my attention to an interview in the Department-level press, in which Eliot bemoaned the cancer-fueled insanity that had led his mother to refuse to come back, and bewailed at length how he could do nothing else, it was his mother, after all, nothing but that could ever induce him, *etcetera. etcetera.*

Eliot almost replied, but managed to stop himself, and he spoke only to his parents during the meal, actually forcing us to pass offers of more this or that through them.

"Is not-Uncle Eliot okay, Mummy?" asked Polly, after watching this curiously for a while. "He's acting funny."

Luc positively sniggered and got in before me. "He's *not speaking* to us, Polly."

"But he's older than Daddy, isn't he?"

"I know," snorted Luc.

"Luc," I said sternly.

"Sorry, Mummy," he giggled. "I've just never seen a *grown-up* do that before!"

I sighed. Eliot glowered, but the next time Bane offered him the cauliflower, he muttered a reply.

I'd just brought out the pudding when there was a knock on the door. I was already on my feet, so went to get it. Friedrich and Calla. I let them in.

"Mrs. Verrall, you won't believe... Oh, I'm sorry. You've got guests."

"It's all right. Was there something you wanted to tell us?"

Friedrich shot a look at the busy table, but seemed unable to keep the news in. "Calla has agreed to marry me!"

That brought all activity from Bane, Jon, and the children to a sudden halt. I was just as flabbergasted. "Calla has...? But... are you...? I didn't even know you were dating!"

Friedrich was blushing. Calla might have been too, but her skin was so very dark it was hard to tell.

"Well, we kept it quiet," said Friedrich. "You know Calla has a bit of a reputation for, you know, not being in a relationship, and... what with my history... we were worried we'd get far too much attention. That it would feel like a lot of pressure. So we kept it low profile."

It was all I could do not to whistle. To manage to hold a courtship right up to the point of getting engaged, without it becoming common knowledge, *here?* That was quite a feat. Well, I'd known for a long time that Friedrich wasn't as dumb as he sometimes came across—he'd had a successful career as an undercover agent, after all—and Calla, for all her lack of zeal for bodyguarding, was an extremely astute desk agent.

"To be honest," said Calla, "I think U figured it out, but you know him. Perfect gentleman; wasn't going to let on. And we had to tell Eduardo, but like anyone's getting anything out of *him.*"

"And now we're engaged, so we're happy to tell people at last!" said Friedrich.

And he'd come to me first because over the years, despite him being older than me, he'd come to see me as a bit of a mother figure. Since I was pretty sure he'd had a huge crush on me initially, this wasn't something I felt like complaining about. "Wow. Wow, I'm so happy for you both. You must come in and have a drink and a slice of pudding. Children, can you sit on the sofa, please?"

The children slowly decamped, via Calla and their Uncle Georg, who they hugged and danced around and congratulated with a considerable amount of noise, but finally our two extra guests were seated at the table.

"Georg and Calla have just got engaged," I reiterated, for the benefit of the non-Vatican residents, as Bane reappeared with a bottle of wine and tray of glasses.

Mrs. Marsden stared wide-eyed from German Friedrich—pale skin and blond hair—to African Calla—dark dark skin and black hair—but said, "Oh, ah... Congratulations, both of you."

Mr. Marsden sniffed and said nothing.

Eliot gave them a look of total disgust and positively declaimed, "Good grief, have you no *shame?*"

Calla, born and bred in Africa, looked faintly puzzled for a moment, then scowled; Friedrich flushed with anger, and shot me a look which I decoded easily enough as, 'Please may I pull out my nonLee and shoot your guest?'

I gave him a tiny head shake. "I apologize for Eliot," I said. "He works for the EuroGov but hasn't kept up with the times."

"What *shame?*" asked Luc and Polly, peering over the back of the sofa.

"There's no shame," Bane said firmly. "It's very, very happy news. Here we go; I've got the cork out." He poured wine for everyone, an eggcupful for Luc, and supervised a sip for Polly from his own glass. When he peeped over the sofa and returned to his place smiling, I surmised that Javi had curled up and gone to sleep.

"To Calla and Georg," said Jon, raising his glass. "Lord, please bless them with a long and happy life together!"

"Amen!" we all chorused. Well, everyone who had their glass raised. *What a ray of light that was.*

And so, quite unexpectedly the evening turned into a lively affair—despite Eliot's disapproving presence.

7ᵗʰ October (26)

Bane's mum is stuck in bed, now. So frail, it's like she's turning into cobweb. Doctor Frederick has brought some equipment down to her room so she doesn't have to go to the hospital wing. Bane spends every moment he can with her. They talk much more easily now. Eliot lurks, mostly, and makes nasty remarks, but they ignore those.

9ᵗʰ October (26)   *THANKS BE TO GOD!*

Mrs. Marsden got baptized today. Bane and Luc are so happy. Mr. Marsden just seemed resigned. His antagonistic attitude is slipping into perpetual bewilderment. I'm actually starting to feel a bit sorry for him. As for Eliot, he was so shocked, he forgot to be obnoxious for the rest of the day.

11ᵗʰ October (26)

Bane and I went to see Doctor Carol, today. Bane had asked if I minded if we found out the baby's sex. We were going to wait and see, but it was clear it was suddenly quite important to him, so I said I didn't mind. It's a girl! Bane would like to call her Portia Elizabeth, after both our mothers. He wants to tell his mum, you see, that's why he didn't want to wait. *I hope you didn't really mind, Margo.*

No. Truth be told, I was thinking of suggesting we find out anyway.

12ᵗʰ October (26)

Eliot finally asked me about Kyle, today. In an angry sort of way, but he asked. I told him he's got a parish in

Africa and is really happy, and he wishes he could come and see Eliot while he's here but doesn't think he can get away, so would Eliot speak to him on the phone? Eliot made huffs and puffs worthy of an ancient steam engine, and totally dismissed the idea, but you never know. One day, maybe.

Bane told Mrs. Marsden about the baby's name. She cried, she was so happy. I'm really glad Bane thought of it. So am I.

20ᵗʰ October (26)

So it finally happened, today, in the early hours of the morning. It was very peaceful. Bane and Eliot and Mr. Marsden were all with her, and me and the children. Jon was there too, at her request, as a priest. Eliot hadn't been mean to Bane in front of her for about three days, which made her very happy, I think, though a lot of the time she wasn't conscious. But she finally slipped away.

I was afraid Eliot and Mr. Marsden would get really savage, once she was gone, but they asked for the funeral to be held today — she said she wanted to be buried here — and then they left straight afterwards, very quietly, without saying much.

We told them they're welcome to come and visit the grave whenever they like, and they didn't say that they were never going to set foot here again, even for that. They didn't say they'd be coming, either, but I can't help wondering if that's part of why she asked to be buried here. In the hope it might keep up that connection. So that maybe, one day, they might thaw too.

Bane's really upset to have lost her, having just kind of found her, but she was so ill by the end, I think it's a bit of a relief too. Doctor Frederick was having to give her medication just to help her breathe properly. The children are sad, of course, although Luc and Polly knew it was coming. Javi didn't really get that, because he's still asking for other-Granny. Breaks my heart, that does.

I think the fact we parted so peacefully from Mr. Marsden and Eliot was a real comfort to Bane, though. After all, while there's life, there's hope, right? I s'pose so.

Anyway, I'm almost out of space in this diary, but there's one page left and I realize I've never copied out that hymn I chose for Lucas's funeral! It's such a favorite of mine and I always meant to. Since Bane chose it for his mum's funeral, I can't think of anything more appropriate with which to end this diary of mine:

Neither can I. Thanks, Margo.

You're very welcome.

xxx

Now the Green Blade Riseth

Now the green blade riseth from the buried grain,
Wheat that in dark earth many years has lain;
Love lives again, that with the dead has been:
    Love is come again,
    like wheat that springeth green.

In the grave they laid Him, Love Whom men had slain,
Thinking that never He would wake again,
Laid in the earth like grain that sleeps unseen:
    Love is come again,
    like wheat that springeth green.

Forth He came at Easter, like the risen grain,
He that for three days in the grave had lain,
Quick from the dead my risen Lord is seen:
    Love is come again,
    like wheat that springeth green.

When our hearts are wintry, grieving, or in pain,
Thy touch can call us back to life again,
Fields of our hearts that dead and bare have been:
    Love is come again,
    like wheat that springeth green.

J. M. C. Crum (1872–1958)

Bee did me this lovely picture of the Swiss Guard
Graveyard where Snakey is buried, so I thought I would
stick it safely in here. They got Bee into art for
therapeutic reasons, but he's really good! He mostly does
it on a special Graphics NetworkAccessor. He has lots of
different styluses!

'ProCamera Mass kit Mark 7.0'

This is a diagram of a secret Mass kit, like the priests used to carry. They never made two the same, for obvious reasons, but this is the one I'm most familiar with.

Might as well call it a: ─────

If you really MINDED, you wouldn't leave it open on my pillow!

Groan! Margo, that's a terrible pun!
I'm in physical pain now!
Don't read my diary, then!

⊿───── So the base unit is a real camera. They used to use all sorts of things, always genuine; anything they could adapt. Shaving kits, laptops, I even saw one fitted into a bookReader once!

Inside the innocent looking modem battery pack, are two vials, disguised as small antique batteries, just to confuse any searcher even more!

You should know about that! It really freaked me out, that did! "It's only for sick people." Hmm!

Well, Fr Mark was telling the truth! It is for sick people! HMMM!

They actually contain Holy Water and Holy Oil for the Anointing of the Sick!

The lenses! These are the important part. The inner one holds communion wine, the outer one the hosts. The lens itself unscrews to allow access to a compartment large enough to hold one precious consecrated Host, allowing the priest to keep one for emergencies (if considered wise) but be able to access and consume it almost instantly if threatened with discovery/desecration.

Fr Mark loved that feature!

This was the most awesome feature of Fr Mark's proCamera! The flash fitted into the lens shade so that it would stand upright, nice and stable. The lens cap pyx had a clear back, and fitted onto the top of the flash. Voila! Monstrance!

It was quite cool, that.
Pleased you remember!

What, you don't remember making me stare at the thing for over half an hour at a time before you'd come and do anything fun? It's seared into my memory, trust me! Of course, I appreciate it properly now...
Glad to hear it!

121

Underground Latin Primer

Why do you need this?

I don't, but I did it for my blog and thought it was fun!

Useful Phrases:
Hello - *Salve*
Goodbye - *Vale*
Thank you - *Gratias tibi ago*
Help! - *Adiuva me!*

Things you may want to say:
What time is Mass? - *Quando Missa est?/quanta hora est Missa?*
What time is breakfast/lunch/dinner? - *Quando ientaculum / prandium / cena est?*
What is the name of that: *quid est nomen illius...*

- Man: *viri?*
- Woman: *mulieri?*
- Priest: *sacerdotis?*
- Bishop: *Episcopi?*
- Cardinal: *Cardinalis?*
- Sister: *sororis?*
- Brother: *fratris?*
- Nun: *monialis?*
- Monk: *monachi?*
- Chicken: *pullus?*

- Swiss Guard: *custodis Helvetiorum Cohortis?*
- Vatican Policeman: *diasostae Vaticanae?*
- Vatican Secret Service Agent?: *otacustae Vaticanae?*

Am I allowed to feed the doves?: *Licet columbas alere?*
The explosives have all been removed, now, right?: *Nonne iam omnes bombae remotae sunt?*
Hello, I'm here to have tea with the Pope. - *Salve, advenisti ut theam cum Papa bibeam*
Could you tell me the way to the:
       Potesne mihi narrare quam viam ferat ad....

- Cafeteria: *cauponam?*
- Sistine Chapel: *capellam Sistinam?*
- St Peters: *Basilicam Sancti Petri?*
- Train Station: *stationem hamoxostichorum?*
- Department Store: *forum?*
- Veritas TV & Radio station: *stationem telehorasis radiophonique Veritatis?*
- Swiss Guard Barracks: *castra Helvetiorum Cohortis?*
- Vatican Police Barracks: *castra diasostrarum Vaticanae?*

- Greenhouses: *conservatoria?*
- Heliport: *heliportem?*
- Smallholding: *agellum?*
- Gardens: *hortos?*

Things people may say to you:
Hello, welcome to Vatican State: *Salve/salvete. Adventu tuo/vestro in Civitatem Vaticanam festum ago.* (If there's one of you/if there's more of you.)
May I see your ID card?: *Syngraphum videam?*
Watch out for that: *Cave...* (to one person.) *Cavete...* (to more than one)
  - low doorway: *limen breve*
  - step: *gradum*
  - dove: *columbam*
  - fuchsia: *fuchsiam/Fuchsias* (singular/plural)
  - assassin: *sicarium/sicarios* (singular/plural)
    Always useful!

Signs/messages you may see:
No Photography: *Nolite photographere*
Keep off the fuchsias: Nolite fuchsias calcare.
ID card declined for purchase - Code E16:
  Codex E sedecim: syngraphus detractatus.
    [E: excessive use; 16: chocolate products] Has this happened to you, Margo?
    Well, you know that time Luc took my card and went to the store? Well, the next time I went in... Hahahahaha! I remember now!

Useful exclamations
  (O) Lord God! *Domine Deus!*
  Praise the Lord: *Laudate Dominum*
  God Almighty: *Deus omnipotens*
  Thank the Lord: *Gratias Domino agimus*
  Deliver us, Lord: *Libera nos, Domine*

Dragon in his Vatican Police uniform
  — by Bee

Some Favorite Psalms.

Some of these are definitely Bible verses.... Pedant!

Psalm 14

To the choirmaster. Of David.

The fool says in his heart, "There is no God."
  They are corrupt, they do abominable deeds, *Read this, EuroGov!*
  there is none that does good.

The Lord looks down from heaven upon the children of men,
    to see if there are any that act wisely,
    that seek after God. *We are trying, Lord. That's certainly true!*

They have all gone astray, they are all alike corrupt;
    there is none that does good,
    no, not one.

Have they no knowledge, all the evildoers
    who eat up My people as they eat bread,
    and do not call upon the Lord? *Or steal their organs or kill their babies...*

There they shall be in great terror,
    for God is with the generation of the righteous.
You would confound the plans of the poor,
    but the Lord is his refuge.

O that deliverance for Israel would come out of Zion!
    When the Lord restores the fortunes of His people,
    Jacob shall rejoice, Israel shall be glad.

There's been a bit of restoring going on in the EuroBloc over the last... whoa, it's not a decade yet, is it? No... 7/8 years? So thank You for that, anyway.

Psalm 143
A psalm. Of David.
Listen, Lord, to my prayer;
give my plea a hearing, as Thou art ever faithful;
listen, Thou who lovest the right.
Do not call Thy servant to account;
what man is there living that can stand guiltless in Thy
presence?   Not me, alas.

See how my enemies plot against my life,
how they have abased me in the dust,
set me down in dark places, like the long-forgotten dead!
My spirits are crushed within me, I don't like this psalm, Margo.
my heart is cowed.

And my mind goes back to past days;
I think of all Thou didst once,
dwell on the proofs Thou gavest of Thy power.
To Thee I spread out my hands in prayer,
for Thee my soul thirsts, like a land parched with
drought.

Hasten, Lord, to answer my prayer;
my spirit grows faint.
Do not turn Thy face away from me,
and leave me like one sunk in the abyss.
Speedily let me win Thy mercy,
my hope is in Thee;
to Thee I lift up my heart,
shew me the path I must follow;
to Thee I fly for refuge,
deliver me, Lord, from my enemies.

Thou art my God,
teach me to do Thy will;
let Thy gracious spirit lead me,
safe ground under my feet.

For the honor of Thy own name, Lord, grant me life;
in Thy mercy rescue me from my cruel affliction. Thanks for
Have pity on me, and scatter my enemies; doing that, Lord.
 thy servant I; (And thanks, Lucas.)
make an end of my cruel persecutors.

Foxie and Trout on duty in St Peter's Square.
By Bee, of course.

Psalm 142 (David in the cave or me in the Facility.)
   A maskil. Of David, when he
     was in the cave. A prayer.
Loud is my cry to the Lord,
the prayer I utter for the Lord's mercy,
as I pour out my complaint before Him,
tell Him of the affliction I endure.
My heart is ready to faint within me,
but Thou art watching over my path.

They lie in ambush for me,
there by the wayside;
I look to the right of me,
and find none to take my part;
all hope of escape is cut off from me,
none is concerned for my safety.

I hope you didn't feel like this in
the Facility, Margo.

I was concerned for your
safety, so were your Mum and
Dad, and Fr Mark.

To Thee, Lord, I cry,
claiming Thee for my only refuge,
all that is left me in this world of living men.
Listen, then, to my plea;
Thou seest me all defenseless.
Rescue me from persecutors
who are too strong for me;
restore liberty to a captive soul.
What thanks, then, will I give to Thy name,
honest hearts all about me,
rejoicing to see Thy favor restored!

I know you were, Bane.
I did know it.
Sometimes it still felt a bit
like this, though.

Psalm 84
Lord of hosts, how I love Thy dwelling-place!
For the courts of the Lord's house,
my soul faints with longing.
The living God! at His name my heart,
my whole being thrills with joy.
Where else should the sparrow find a home,
the swallow a nest for her brood,
but at Thy altar, Lord of hosts,
my king and my God?

*How blessed, Lord, are those who
dwell in Thy house!
They will be ever praising thee.
Happy those whose strength is in You,
people with pilgrim hearts.
As they pass through the valley of tears,
they make it a place of fountains,
clothed with the blessings of early rain.
So, at each stage refreshed,
they will reach Sion,
and have sight there of the God
Who is above all gods.

Lord of hosts, listen to my prayer;
God of Israel, grant me audience!
God, ever our protector, do not disregard us now;
look favorably upon him whom Thou hast anointed!
Willingly would I give a thousand of my days
for one spent in Thy courts! Willingly reach but the
threshold of my God's house,

so I might dwell no more in the abode of sinners!
Sun to enlighten, shield to protect us,
the Lord God has favor, has honor to bestow.
 To innocent lives
He will never refuse His bounty;
Lord of hosts,
blessed is the man who puts his confidence in Thee.

Isaiah 42

The Servant, a Light to the Nations

Here is My servant, whom I uphold,
  My chosen, in whom My soul delights;
I have put My spirit upon him;
  he will bring forth justice to the nations.
He will not cry or lift up his voice,
  or make it heard in the street;
a bruised reed he will not break,
  and a dimly burning wick he will not quench;
  he will faithfully bring forth justice.

A super-nice person, in other words.

He will not grow faint or be crushed
  until he has established justice in the earth;
  and the coastlands wait for his teaching.
Thus says God, the LORD,

It's talking about Our Lord, Bane.

Ah-ha. That makes sense.

  who created the heavens and stretched them out,
  who spread out the earth and what comes from it,
who gives breath to the people upon it
  and spirit to those who walk in it:
I am the LORD, I have called you in righteousness,
  I have taken you by the hand and kept you;
I have given you as a covenant to the people,
  a light to the nations,
  to open the eyes that are blind,
to bring out the prisoners from the dungeon,
  from the prison those who sit in darkness.

OK, I like this psalm!

I am the LORD, that is My name;
  My glory I give to no other,
  nor My praise to idols.
See, the former things have come to pass,
  and new things I now declare;

before they spring forth,
  I tell you of them.

    A Hymn of Praise
Sing to the LORD a new song,
  His praise from the end of the earth!
Let the sea roar and all that fills it,
  the coastlands and their inhabitants.
Let the desert and its towns lift up their voice,
  the villages that Kedar inhabits;
let the inhabitants of Sela sing for joy,
  let them shout from the tops of the mountains.
Let them give glory to the LORD,
  and declare His praise in the coastlands.
The LORD goes forth like a soldier,
  like a warrior He stirs up His fury;
He cries out, He shouts aloud,
  He shows himself mighty against His foes. *Yeah!*
For a long time I have held My peace,
  I have kept still and restrained Myself;
now I will cry out like a woman in labor, *Okay, that's a bit weird...*
  I will gasp and pant.
I will lay waste mountains and hills, *But if all this happens to*
  and dry up all their herbage; *the EuroGov I won't*
I will turn the rivers into islands, *complain...*
  and dry up the pools.
I will lead the blind
  by a road they do not know, *Jon says he really likes*
by paths they have not known *these verses.*
  I will guide them.
I will turn the darkness before them into light,
  the rough places into level ground.

These are the things I will do,
  and I will not forsake them.
They shall be turned back and utterly put to shame –
  those who trust in carved images,
who say to cast images,
  "You are our gods."
Listen, you that are deaf;
  and you that are blind, look up and see!
Who is blind but My servant,
  or deaf like My messenger whom I send?
Who is blind like My dedicated one,
  or blind like the servant of the LORD?
He sees many things, but does not observe them;
  his ears are open, but he does not hear.

The statues from on top of St Peter's. Bee's work.

Psalm 62

To the leader: according to
Jeduthun. A Psalm of David.
For God alone my soul waits in silence;
from Him comes my salvation.
He alone is my rock and my salvation,
my fortress; I shall never be shaken.

How long will you assail a person,
will you batter your victim, all of you,
as you would a leaning wall, a tottering fence?
Their only plan is to bring down a person of prominence.
They take pleasure in falsehood;   Sounds like what the
they bless with their mouths,   EuroGov do to you, Margo.
but inwardly they curse. (Selah)   Yes, I do feel the need to
read this psalm quite often!

For God alone my soul waits in silence,
for my hope is from Him.
He alone is my rock and my salvation,
my fortress; I shall not be shaken.
On God rests my deliverance and my honor;
my mighty rock, my refuge is in God.

Trust in Him at all times, O people;
pour out your heart before Him;
God is a refuge for us. (Selah)

Those of low estate are but a breath,
those of high estate are a delusion;
in the balances they go up;
they are together lighter than a breath.
Put no confidence in extortion,

133

and set no vain hopes on robbery;
  if riches increase, do not set your heart on them.

The EuroGov should read this.

Once God has spoken;
  twice have I heard this:
that power belongs to God,
  and steadfast love belongs to You, O Lord.
For You repay to all
  according to their work.

I'm not sure why Foxie and his older comrade are
    looking quite so put out with Bee, here!

He was torturing them by sketching and
eating an ice-cream, on a VERY hot day!

On purpose? Doesn't
seem like Bee.
Haha, no, inadvertently,
bless him!

Song of Songs 2:8–10, 14, 16; 8:6–7

*I hear my Beloved.
See how he comes
leaping on the mountains,
bounding over the hills.*

Our perfect wedding reading!
I thought it looked
familiar...

Very funny, Bane.

xxx

*My Beloved is like a gazelle,
like a young stag.
See where he stands
behind our wall.*

*He looks in at the window,
he peers through the lattice.
My Beloved lifts up his voice,
he says to me,
'Come then, my love,
my lovely one, come.*

This rings
a bell...

*My dove, hiding in the clefts of the rock.
In the coverts of the cliff,
show me your face,
let me hear your voice;
for your voice is sweet
and your face is beautiful.'*

My beloved is mine and I am his.

*Set me like a seal on your heart,
like a seal on your arm.*

For love is strong as Death,
jealousy relentless as Sheol.

The flash of it is a flash of fire,
a flame of the Lord himself.
Love no flood can quench,
no torrents drown.

Psalm 111 (Our Wedding Psalm!)
Happy the man who fears the Lord,
who takes delight in His commands.
His sons will be powerful on earth;
the children of the upright are blessed.

Riches and wealth are in his house;
his justice stands firm forever.
He is a light in the darkness for the upright:
he is generous, merciful and just.
The good man takes pity and lends,
he conducts his affairs with honor.
The just man will never waver:
he will be remembered for ever.
He has no fear of evil news;
with a firm heart he trusts in the Lord.
With a steadfast heart he will not fear;
he will see the downfall of his foes.
                                    Hurray!

1 Corinthians 13:1, 3–8 (Our second wedding reading!)

If I have all the eloquence of men or of angels, but speak without love, I am simply a gong booming or a cymbal clashing.

If I give away all that I possess, piece by piece, and if I even let them take my body to burn it, but am without love, it will do me no good whatever.

Love is always patient and kind; it is never jealous; love is never boastful or conceited; it is never rude or selfish; it does not take offence, and is not resentful.

Love takes no pleasure in other people's sins but delights in the truth; it is always ready to excuse, to trust, to hope, and to endure whatever comes.

Love does not come to an end. *Or to summarise: love is awesome – and a whole lot of work.*

Matthew 5:13–16 Our Wedding Gospel! (The one Bane insisted on!)

Jesus said to his disciples: 'You are the salt of the earth. But if salt becomes tasteless, what can make it salty again? It is good for nothing, and can only be thrown out to be trampled underfoot by men.'

'You are the light of the world. A city built on a hill-top cannot be hidden. No one lights a lamp to put it under a tub; they put it on the lamp-stand where it shines for everyone in the house. In the same way your light must shine in the sight of men, so that, seeing your good works, they may give the praise to your Father in heaven.'

Pigeon in his blue everyday uniform.

It's a black and white sketch, Margo!

That's why I wrote 'blue' next to it!

Psalm 112

Hallelujah. Happy are those who fear the LORD,
  and greatly delight in His commandments.
Mighty on earth shall be their seed;
  a blessing shall rest on the race of the upright.
Wealth and riches are in their houses,
  their prosperity stands forever.
To the upright arises light in the darkness;
  full of favor and pity and kindness are they.
It is well with those who show pity and lend,
  who support all their affairs upon justice.
For they will never be shaken;
  the just will be forever remembered.
They will not be afraid of evil tidings,
  with steady heart they trust the LORD.
Their heart is firm and unafraid:
  they know they will feast their eyes on their enemies.
With lavish hands they give to the poor,
and their prosperity stands forever.
  They are lifted to heights of triumph and honor.
The sight of them fills the wicked with anger:
  grinding their teeth with despair.
  The hopes of the wicked will come to nothing.

Always a very encouraging psalm.

Anything about 'light in darkness' gets my vote!

Changing of the guard. On a cold winter's day, looking at their big BLUE cloaks!

Psalm 88 – The Prayer of Despair
O Lord my God,
   I cry for help in the day-time,
   in the night my cry is before You;
let my prayer come into Your presence,
   incline Your ear to my cry.

 For I am sated with sorrow,
   my life draws near to Sheol.
I am counted with those who go down to the pit;
   without strength am I.

My home is among the dead,
   like the slain that lie in the grave,
whom You remember no more
   cut off as they are from Your hand.

In the deepest pit You have put me,
   in shadows deep and dark.
Your wrath lies heavy upon me,
   waves of Your anger roll over me. (Selah)

You have put my friends far from me,
   You have made them shun me.
I am shut in, and cannot escape,
   my eyes are wasted with sorrow.
I call on You, Lord, every day,
   spreading my hands out to You.

I can never read
this one without
remembering how
much it always upset
Lucas. He felt like it
described his life
completely, or at
least his experience
of life.

For the dead can You work wonders?
   Can the shades rise again to praise You? (Selah)
Can Your kindness be told in the grave,

Your faithfulness in the tomb?
Can Your wonders be known in the darkness,
    or Your help in the land of forgetfulness?

I cry for help to You,
    in the morning my prayer comes before You.
Why, O Lord, do you spurn me,
    and hide Your face from me?
From my youth I am wretched and dying,
    I am numbed by the terrors I bear.

The fires of Your wrath have passed over me,
    Your terrors destroy me,
surging around me forever,
    hemming me in altogether.
Those who love me You put far from me;
    the dark is my only friend.

For the record, Margo, I HATE it too!

John 15.9–17

"As the Father has loved me, so have I loved you;
remain in my love. If you lay my commands to heart, you
will remain in my love; just as I have laid the Father's
commands to heart and remain in His love. I have told
you all this so that my own joy may be yours, and that
your joy may be complete."

"This is my command — love one another, as I have
loved you. No one can give greater proof of love than by
laying down their life for their friends. And you are my
friends, if you do what I command you. I no longer call
you 'servants,' because a servant does not know what their

master is doing; but I have given you the name of 'friends', because I made known to you everything that I learned from my Father. It wasn't you who chose me, but I who chose you, and I appointed you to go and bear fruit — fruit that should remain, so that the Father might grant you whatever you ask in my name. I am giving you these commands that you may love one another." *RIP Snakey, much missed!*

   And after <u>that</u> reading I must stick in this picture: St Peter's on the left and the Swiss Guard Graveyard on the right, or as its real official name is: 'Campo Santo Teutonico' (not that anyone uses it).

Luke 2:29-32
"Now, Lord, You will let Your servant go,
   According to Your word, in peace,   *And Fr Mark,*
for my eyes have seen the salvation   *very much ditto.*
Which You have prepared in the sight of all nations —
A light to bring light to the Gentiles,
   And to be the glory of Your people Israel."

Psalm 4 – Confident Plea for Deliverance from Enemies
    To the choirmaster: with stringed
    instruments. A Psalm of David.
Answer me when I call, O God of my right!
   Thou hast given me room when I was in distress.
   Be gracious to me, and hear my prayer.

O men, how long shall my honor suffer shame?
   How long will you love vain words, and seek after lies?
                                                    (Selah)

But know that the LORD has set apart the godly for
Himself;
   the LORD hears when I call to Him. *You seem to mostly have the very comforting psalms in here, Margo.*

Be angry, but sin not;
   commune with your own hearts on your beds, and be
silent. (Selah)
Offer right sacrifices,   *Well, it's not like anything has ever
   and put your trust in the LORD.   happened in my life that might
                                            make me very
                                   fond of comforting psalms, is it?
                                                    Hahahahaha!*
There are many who say, "O that we might see some
good!
   Lift up the light of Thy countenance upon us, O LORD!"
Thou hast put more joy in my heart
   than they have when their grain and wine abound.

In peace I will both lie down and sleep;
   for Thou alone, O LORD, makest me dwell in safety.

Psalm 146 – The Great Protector

My soul, praise the LORD.
  I will praise the LORD, while I live;
I will sing to my God, while I am.

Put not your trust in princes
  mortals, in whom is no help.
When their breath goes out,
  they go back to the dust:
on that very day their purposes perish.

Happy those whose help
  is the God of Jacob:
whose hope is set
  on the LORD their God,
the Creator of heaven and earth,
  the sea, and all that is in them.

He remains eternally loyal.
  For the wronged He executes justice;
He gives bread to the hungry;
  the LORD releases the prisoners.
The LORD gives sight to the blind:
  the LORD raises those who are bowed.
The LORD loves the righteous.
  The LORD preserves the stranger,
upholds the widow and orphan,
  but the wicked he leads to disaster.

The LORD shall reign forever,
  your God, O Zion, to all generations.
Hallelujah.

Isaiah 1:18
Come now, let us set things right, says the LORD:
Though your sins be like scarlet,
    they may become white as snow;
Though they be red like crimson,
    they may become white as wool.

Fr Mark loved these verses. So did Lucas.

I quite like them too.

Matthew 18:21-35
    The Parable of the Unforgiving Servant.
Then Peter approaching asked him, "Lord, if my brother
sins against me, how often must I forgive him? As many
as seven times?"

And here's another favourite of them both...

    Jesus answered, "I say to you, not seven times but
seventy-seven times. That is why the kingdom of heaven
may be likened to a king who decided to settle accounts
with his servants. When he began the accounting, a debtor
was brought before him who owed him a huge
amount. Since he had no way of paying it back, his master
ordered him to be sold, along with his wife, his children,
and all his property, in payment of the debt.
    "At that, the servant fell down, did him homage, and
said, 'Be patient with me, and I will pay you back in
full.' Moved with compassion the master of that servant let
him go and forgave him the loan.
    "When that servant had left, he found one of his
fellow servants who owed him a much smaller amount. He
seized him and started to choke him, demanding, 'Pay
back what you owe.'
    "Falling to his knees, his fellow servant begged him, 'Be
patient with me, and I will pay you back.' But he refused.

Instead, he had him put in prison until he paid back the debt.

"Now when his fellow servants saw what had happened, they were deeply disturbed, and went to their master and reported the whole affair.

"His master summoned him and said to him, 'You wicked servant! I forgave you your entire debt because you begged me to. Should you not have had pity on your fellow servant, as I had pity on you?'

"Then in anger his master handed him over to the torturers until he should pay back the whole debt.

"So will my heavenly Father do to you, unless each of you forgives his brother from his heart."

Important Prayers:

Act of Acceptance
O Lord, I now, at this moment,
accept whatever kind of death
it may please You to send me,
with all its pains and sorrows.

I hope you don't need this one anymore, Margo!

Believers will always need this one.

Well, that's cheerful.

Prayer to St Michael the Archangel
Holy Michael, the Archangel, defend us in battle.
Be our safeguard against the wickedness and snares of
  the devil.
May God rebuke him, we humbly pray;
and do you, O Prince of the heavenly host,
by the power of God cast into hell Satan
and all the evil spirits who wander through the world
seeking the ruin of souls. Amen.

I prefer THIS ONE.

What a surprise.
xxx

Dove on guard, in his full ceremonial uniform.

Not quite, Margo.. No armour!

Okay, but he's not in his everyday blues.

Bee did me this awesome picture of Veritas
TV & Radio. (Seeing that I spend so
much time there) It's one of the most
unmistakeable Vatican buildings – impossible to
miss!

Something about
the huge
transmitter on top,
do you think?
You know, it
might just be.

148

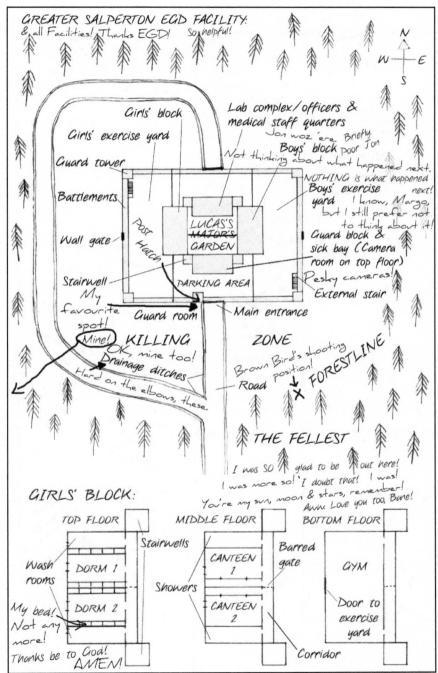

GREATER SALPERTON EGD FACILITY:
& all Facilities! Thanks EGD! So helpful!

N W E S

Girls' block

Girls' exercise yard

Lab complex / officers & medical staff quarters
Jon woz 'ere. Briefly.
Boys' block Poor Jon
Not thinking about what happened next.

Guard tower

Battlements

Wall gate

Post Hatch

LUCAS'S ~~MAJOR'S~~ GARDEN

NOTHING is what happened next!
Boys' exercise yard I know, Margo, but I still prefer not to think about it!

Guard block & sick bay (Camera room on top floor)
Pesky cameras!
External stair

Stairwell
My favourite spot!
Mine! OK, mine too!

PARKING AREA

Guard room

Main entrance

KILLING   ZONE
Drainage ditches
Hard on the elbows, these.

Brown Bird's shooting position!
Road   X FORESTLINE

THE FELLEST

I was SO glad to be out here!
I was more so! `I doubt that! I was!
You're my sun, moon & stars, remember!
Aww. Love you too, Bane!

GIRLS' BLOCK:

TOP FLOOR

Stairwells

Wash rooms

DORM 1

DORM 2

My bed! Not any more!
Thanks be to God! AMEN!

MIDDLE FLOOR

CANTEEN 1

Showers

CANTEEN 2

Barred gate

Corridor

BOTTOM FLOOR

GYM

Door to exercise yard

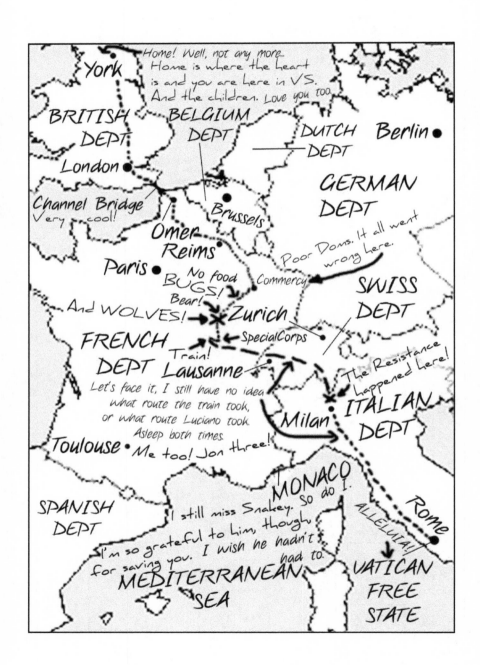

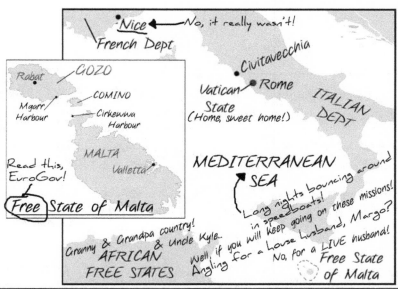

Nice ← No, it really wasn't!
French Dept

GOZO
Rabat
COMINO
Mgarr Harbour
Cirkewwa Harbour
MALTA
Valletta

Read this, EuroGov!
Free State of Malta

Civitavecchia
Vatican State (Home, sweet home!) — Rome
ITALIAN DEPT

MEDITERRANEAN SEA

Long nights bouncing around in speedboats! And you will keep going on these missions! Angling for a house husband, Margo? No, for a LIVE husband!

Granny & Grandpa country! & Uncle Kyle...
AFRICAN FREE STATES

Free State of Malta

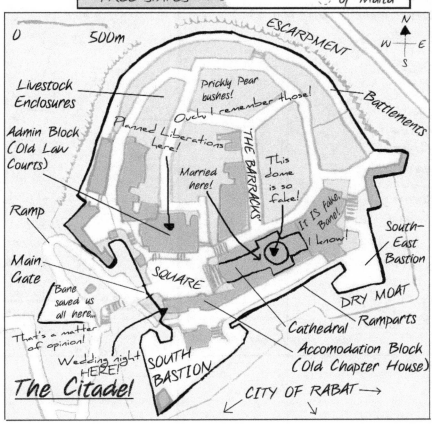

0   500m

ESCARPMENT

N
W   E
S

Livestock Enclosures

Prickly Pear bushes!
Ouch! I remember those!

Battlements

Admin Block (Old Law Courts)

Planned Liberations here!

Married here!

THE BARRACKS

This dome is so fake!

It IS fake, Bane! I know!

Ramp

South-East Bastion

Main Gate

Bane saved us all here...

SQUARE

That's a matter of opinion!

DRY MOAT

Ramparts

Wedding night HERE!

SOUTH BASTION

Cathedral

Accomodation Block (Old Chapter House)

The Citadel

CITY OF RABAT →

With annotations by Bane

They're so-so, here!

RussianBloc

So big it needs two labels!

OceanicBloc

OceanicBloc

Horrible place to live!

EuroBloc

ArabOil Bloc

Keep to themselves.

AFRICAN FREE STATES

To think we were expecting to spend our lives in the A.F.S. and we still haven't even set foot there!

Mediterranean Island + Free States + Vatican Free State

Nice places to live!

USNA.
(United States of North America)

Rather too like the EuroBloc for my taste.

USSA.
(United States of South America)

Pretty good place to live.

Squire Thane and the Dragon
(Bane's story!)

Once upon a time there was a beautiful kingdom far
away, with lush green meadows in summer and clean
white snows in winter. The kingdom was ruled by a
good king, and all lived in peace and prosperity until, one
terrible day, a mighty dragon arrived in the land. It
burned crops and villages, and killed livestock. But its
favorite food of all was people. That's unfortunate.
Many innocent peasants were devoured, and
everyone cried to the king to save them from the beast.
But the king was a man advanced in years, and his son
and heir had set off on a fantastic voyage of discovery
and might not return for many years. So the king
appealed to his lords to offer what aid and protection
they could to their people. Delegation at its best!
One of the lords who rose to his king's challenge
was Lord Veritas. He had a beautiful daughter called
Marigold, who busied herself organizing practical
assistance, whilst her father trained his knights and
squires and led them in brave attempts to fend off the
dragon, though with very limited success. Oh dear.
Among Lord Veritas's squires was a young man
called Thane. He was Marigold's age, and his family,
although just-about noble, were of low rank, and very
poor. They had scraped together the means to send
Thane to Lord Veritas as a squire, but there was no
hope of him ever being knighted. He was clearly
doomed to be one of those men who remained a squire

forever, which was a shame because he was a brave and skilled fighter, and intelligent too. Well, that sucks.

It was twice the shame, because Thane was in love with Marigold. Of course, even becoming a knight might not have been enough to win her hand, for she was sure to be bestowed on another powerful lord like her father, but as a squire he could not even hope. Poor Thane.

It was all three times the shame, because Marigold was also in love with Thane. But they both kept quiet about their feelings, because the problems seemed insurmountable. Marigold prayed hard, and concentrated on helping the homeless peasants, and Thane threw himself into his training for all he was worth. You know, I really identify with Thane.

One night, on the feast day of St George, after they'd all listened to a skilled bard sing a tale of doomed love, Thane plucked up the courage to dance with Marigold. Thane had been a squire at the castle for years, now, and they knew each other well. But they still felt awkward to be so close, to be touching...

"That was a sad story, wasn't it," Marigold remarked, trying to distract herself from a rather unchaste thought as Thane's hand rested on her waist. Marigold, really!

"Yes," Thane agreed. "But it could all have been avoided if..." emboldened by his own surging feelings, he went on, "if they'd just run away together." Good idea.

Marigold fought down a deep longing. "How could she, Thane? She was a princess, and her people needed her. You can't just run out on a responsibility like that." Well, this sounds oddly familiar... Quite sure you don't have the gift of prophecy, Margo?

And Thane understood quite clearly that although she wasn't a princess, she felt just as duty-bound to stay. Heavy-hearted, they both finished the dance, in silence, and parted company. *Thane really depressed, now.*

But when the dancing was over, Marigold went to the chapel to pray. "If my feelings for Thane are pure, and his for me," she prayed, "please show me how we can be together." *Yes, please do...*

And that night she had a dream. And she knew what they had to do. *Good job or this story would go nowhere....*

Speaking to Thane in private wasn't easy to achieve. And it could have serious consequences for her — for them both — if anyone caught them. But there was no way to say what had to be said and discuss what had to be discussed in a quick, casual, public conversation. So she slipped a note into his hand as they passed on the stairs, asking him to meet her in the chapel at midnight, and at a few minutes to the appointed time, she crept from her room, tiptoeing past her sleeping maids — whom she'd made sure to keep extra busy in the hope they would sleep more deeply. *Very cunning, Marigold!*

She knelt to pray whilst she waited, and she prayed hard. Her plan was dangerous, and she was terrified she might simply get the man she loved killed. But it was their only chance to be together. *No choice, then.*

Finally, Thane crept in. He looked anxious, and kept his distance. "Lady Marigold, I wasn't even sure whether to come... if someone sees us... you'll be disgraced..." *Then you'll have to come live with me in a hovel, somewhere...*

156

"And you'll lose your position, I know," Marigold walked up to him unhesitatingly. "But we have to talk. There's something we have to do." *j a bit dim, here!*

"There is?" *Thane, you sound a bit dim, here!*

"Yes, but it's very dangerous. We have to kill the dragon." *Oh my, I never saw that coming!*

"What? Ah..." Thane's shock gave way to understanding. Of course. If Squire Thane killed the dragon... Squire Thane would not only be Sir Thane in a twinkling of an eye, but Sir Thane would be able to choose any maiden in the kingdom, up to the king's daughter herself. He wanted only Marigold, of course... "Why didn't I think of that? How will we do it? We'd hardly be the first to try..." *You really should have thought of that, Thane!*

"We'll have to think of a way. Something smarter than running up to it with a sword and hacking at it. That clearly doesn't work. We need to be clever. Set a trap." *Clever Marigold. I really like her.*

"Yes... I hunted a lot with traps as a child. A trap for a dragon would have to be big... but in theory... Why not?"

"We'll both come up with some ideas, then. And Thane?"

"Yes?"

"Let me help?" *No!*

Thane bit his lip. He wanted to say no, but he respected Marigold and knew she had the right to decide for herself. "Let's see if two people are needed," he said. "But if they are..." He nodded reluctantly.

Marigold beamed. She took his hands and squeezed them. He kissed them both, and drew her closer...
Naughty Thane!

Unbeknown to Thane and Marigold, they were not alone. One of the king's courtiers had arrived a few days previously, ostensibly to see how things were going, but Lord Cavil was not what he seemed. Lord Cavil was in fact a sorcerer. In point of fact, Lord Cavil was the one who had lured the dragon to the kingdom in the first place. He hoped the creature's rampaging would destabilize the king's rule, and give him a chance to seize power. Was his name Reginald Cavil?

Recently, he'd discovered something even better. A sorcerous rite that would make him the dragon's master. The thought made him salivate. Once he controlled the dragon, his enemies would fall before him and burn like straw dolls. The king would die... Boo!

But he needed to sacrifice a maiden to the dragon as part of his big sorcery, and Marigold's name was on the list of possible candidates. He was anxious to get it right, since sacrificing a non-maiden by accident would make the whole spell go disastrously wrong. So needless-to-say, as he prowled the castle looking for materials for his dark rite, he was disappointed when he saw Marigold go into the chapel, shortly followed by Thane. Mentally, he scratched her name off the list, wondering idly if the choice of location for the assignation indicated a level of depravity that would make her a suitable recruit for his dark arts. You wish, Cav-hill!

But when he slipped into the sacristy to eavesdrop – information was information, after all, and blackmail could be so much fun – he heard something rather different to what he was expecting. These silly young people planned to kill his dragon! But they had the

158

sense to think of building a trap. Something would have
to be done...   In other words, not so silly at all,
                                    Cav-hill.

Marigold pulled gently away as Thane tried to
draw her closer. He released her hands at once,
flushing in the candlelight. "I'm sorry," he apologized.
    "You know we must not," said Marigold softly.
    "I know. I'm sorry," he said again. "I'll... I'll come up
with a plan."   Be glad it's only a dragon, mate, not a
    "So will I."   fortress full of guards!
    They parted quickly, and hurried from the chapel.
In the sacristy, Cavil was beaming. Contrary to his
expectations, he'd just found a maiden he could be sure
of. And she needed killing anyway. How... neat.
    Don't you know villains always get their comeuppance?
    A couple of days later a servant came to Marigold's
room and handed her a sealed note. She recognized the
handwriting as Thane's, and closed the door before
opening it. Because she's clever...

Dear Lady Marigold,

The perfect opportunity has arisen to achieve what
we discussed. But we must act now! I have gone
ahead to prepare things, but I cannot do it without you.
Please meet me at the beast's place as soon as you
possibly can. Don't delay, we will only get one chance!

Yours forever,

Squire Thane

Without even stopping to change into a riding habit, Marigold raced to the stables and saddled her beautiful grey mare, Truth. She leapt onto her back and rode like the wind, out of the castle and off towards the dragon's lair.

Thane saw her ride out, but since he was on sentry duty, he couldn't do anything about it. As soon as his watch ended, he rushed up to her room and found the letter tucked under her pillow. He read it in bewilderment, then ran for the stables himself, terror gripping him.

For he had not written the letter. *Uh oh...*

Marigold reached the vicinity of the dragon's lair and slowed Truth to a walk. The mare snorted nervously, but kept going forward, so hopefully the dragon was not at home. All the same, Marigold was starting to panic when she saw Thane stick his head between two rocks and beckon to her. She dismounted and led Truth after Thane.

"Tie her up here," said Thane, nodding to where his own mount was tethered.

Marigold did so, and followed him again. They were very close to the lair when Thane stopped. He'd driven a post deep into the ground in the bottom of a rocky dell. He led Marigold to it and grabbed a rope from the ground.

"Quickly!" he said, winding it around her wrists, "before the beast comes..."

"What's the plan?" Marigold asked, not objecting, since, after all, it was Thane and she'd trust him with her life.

"You're the bait," said Thane, binding her firmly to the post. "I've got a trap prepared — the dragon will be looking at you, it won't stand a chance."

"That... sounds clever, but... what if it breathes fire? I mean, wouldn't it be better to use the horses as bait?" Marigold loved Truth, but if one of them had to get cooked...

"This will work better," said Thane dismissively. "Right, you're nice and secure, now I'll set the trap for the dragon."

He grabbed some colored chalk and a handful of curious objects and began to mark strange symbols all over the floor of the dell, radiating out from a spot just in front of the post, placing the objects at various fixed points. Anyone else got a bad feeling about this?

Marigold watched him, unease gathering in her belly. "Thane, what sort of trap is this?"

"Oh, don't worry, it will work. The dragon will land here... it's the obvious spot, and while it's busy eating you, I'll invoke the spell that will bind it to my will. I will be quite the most powerful man in the world."

Marigold stared at him. He didn't appear to be joking, not that it was the sort of joke she would expect from Thane. But some subtle sense of wrongness finally burst fully into her awareness. "You're not Thane," she said. It sounded crazy, even to her, because he looked just like Thane, but... "You're not Thane!" She said it with absolute certainty, and Cavil's illusion spell snapped.

"Ooh, look at the pure maiden, breaking my spells," he sneered. "Well, it would have been entertaining to watch you die thinking I was dear Thane, but it makes no practical difference, unless your certainty can snap those ropes!" And laughing, he put the last few items into place.   *Someone please kill him already!*

Marigold twisted and struggled, but unfortunately Cavil was right. All the pure feeling in the world wouldn't help her get loose.

Cavil ignored her, picking up an old scroll and going over his lines. He was still engrossed when Marigold saw a tiny twin spiral of smoke drifting up over the edge of the hollow. Her mouth went dry. Dragonsmoke. The gentle smoke of a sleeping dragon... or a stalking dragon. And since it was moving...

Cavil had his back to the smoke. Apparently the dragon wasn't going to follow his plan and swoop obligingly down into the hollow and land on the exact spot he'd selected. It was creeping up to see what was what.

Marigold felt in a quandary. If she alerted Cavil to the dragon, he might end up pulling his plan off. Then she'd not only be eaten, but Cavil would be lord of the dragon. But if she distracted Cavil long enough, maybe she'd only end up eaten... No!

So long as Cavil kept reading his scroll, that was fine, no need to speak... She tried not to look straight at those spirals of smoke as they came closer. But Cavil was rolling up his scroll and putting it away. What if he looked around the rim of the dell, and saw the smoke? It was unobtrusive, but she'd spotted it...

"So, how does this work?" she demanded. "Are you sure you need me?"

Cavil laughed at her again. "Nice try, my little petticoat, but yes, I need you."

162

"Why?" demanded Marigold, keeping her eyes firmly on Cavil as the smoke came closer.

"Because a pure maiden must be sacrificed to the dragon in order to feed the sorcery. Since you were up to no good anyway, this is really very economical, don't you think?"

"I suppose so," said Marigold, hardly aware what she was saying, because at the periphery of her vision she could now see a great scaly head appearing silently over the rise. If the beast breathed fire, they'd both be cooked... "Don't you..." she groped frantically for words, her heart hammering, "Don't you think it might be better to keep me for ransom, and choose some lowlier maid?" She felt revolted just saying something like that, but if Cavil looked around now, who knew what would happen.

Cavil just laughed some more. Two scaly forelegs had made it over the rise now. The dragon's head turned from side to side, inspecting them.

Marigold was feeling just a tiny bit bad about keeping her mouth shut, even if he was a foul evil sorcerer. She'd give him one last chance... "Are you sure you wouldn't like to... er... repent?" she suggested. "I think... I think it would be a very good idea if you repented. Right now. And untied me." Good plan, Cav-hill!

Cavil found this so funny he was bending over clutching his stomach when a shadow fell over him. His head snapped up, just in time to get a look into the massive mouth full of massive teeth that was closing over his head. His scream was immediately muffled by the closing jaws. He kicked and struggled and thumped at the dragon's nose—the dragon bit down hard, fangs

163

sinking deep into Cavil's shoulders, then whipped its head from side to side, smacking the man into the nearby crags as a fisherman dispatches a flailing fish. When it opened its mouth and let Cavil's bloody body fall to the ground, he lay still. Comeuppance comeupped!

Marigold wanted to look away, but then she wouldn't know what the dragon was doing. She concentrated on breathing very slowly and quietly, and not moving a single muscle. To no avail. The dragon stepped up to the post, its huge nostrils flaring, and examined her. Marigold gripped her rosary ever so tightly, praying silently, and very hard, since it was clearly one of those situations where praying is all one can do. I REALLY hate those situations.

But, apparently satisfied that its dessert wasn't going anywhere, the dragon stepped back over to Cavil's body, sucked in a deep breath, then blew a steady stream of fire all over it.

As the flames poured past her, Marigold turned her head away from the blazing heat and somehow managed not to scream. Since the dragon was well known to be able to eat three full-grown humans in one meal, and she was slender and Cavil skinny, she felt little hope it would go away and forget about her, but there was still no point attracting its attention. I should think not!

When Cavil was roasted to its satisfaction, the dragon tucked in. Marigold tried not to watch, but again, it was hard not to keep looking at the dragon, to see what it was doing. The beast certainly wasn't wasteful, that was for sure. It ate every scrap of Cavil, leaving only a litter of scorched clothes and a pair of lightly gnawed boots. Marigold began to feel extremely

164

sick, and tried very hard to hold it in. Vomiting was
most un-ladylike, and anyway, it would remind the
dragon of her existence.

As though it had forgotten, she thought resignedly,
as, Cavil's last bones crunched up, it got to its feet and
moved towards her again, sniffing and licking its mighty
jaws. She prayed some more as the jaws opened... it was
going to grab her the way it had grabbed Cavil, rip
her from the stake and smash her...

"Oh no, you don't!"

Finally!

Marigold's head whipped around as Thane rushed
into the clearing, sword in hand. He'd been hoping to
make the most of the element of surprise, but since
Marigold was about to go into the beast's mouth, he
had to make do with hacking at its tail, which was the
only bit he could reach in time. *Weren't you listening to
Marigold earlier?*

The dragon roared and spun around, knocking Thane
flying as it lashed out with its uninjured tail—the scales
had been too thick to penetrate. Thane managed to roll
back onto his feet, and rushed forward again, but the
dragon lunged for him at once. *Told you so.*

Making the split-second calculation that there was
no escape in any direction other than *under,* Thane
dived forward underneath the beast itself. And as the
creature's head came down between its own forelegs, he
drove his sword up into the soft belly, and — since it
penetrated! — rammed it in to the hilt. Snarling and
gasping in pain, the beast lunged in at him, jaws snapping,
sucking in breath to breathe fire...

Thane dragged the sword right across the dragon's
belly as he took shelter behind its own leg. Slimy organs

poured down behind him as he turned his face away, bracing for the flames... *So, covered in dragon innards, now?! Attractive!*

The dragon roared, its jaws so close to Thane's head that he felt his eardrums burst. But the sword had done its work and, eviscerated, the beast began to topple. *Go Thane!*

Thane rolled frantically to his feet and ran. The huge body obliterated where he'd been lying, but Thane wasn't interested in that. He kept right on running to where Marigold was struggling to free herself.

"That's the last time I go riding without my spurs!" she told him. "I could've cut my way out of here by now..."

Thane ignored her grumbles. He couldn't hear properly anyway. He whipped out a dagger and freed her. "Marigold?" He could hardly hear *himself*. "Are you all right?"

"Oh, I'm fine. At least I had my rosary."

Thane thought of all the things he wanted to say to her. The way he felt about her, he wanted to do everything just right. Could he get down on one knee without losing his balance and would he be able to hear what she said in reply...? *And would she mind the innards?*

Apparently not!

Then Marigold's arms wrapped around him like vines around their supporting tree. And when she kissed him, he knew the answer to all his questions was a heartfelt,

'Yes.'

So he never actually got to say, 'Will you marry me?' but they lived happily ever after all the same...

THE END

166

DID YOU WANT TO KNOW WHAT IT WAS FOX AND UNICORN TOLD MARGO?

...The stuff that she didn't think she should write in her diary?

If so, don't forget to go to *www.IAmMargaret.co.uk*
and sign up to receive Corinna Turner's (occasional) newsletters.

You can then access the 'Exclusive Content' page and download the subscriber-only short story:

'How Snakey Got His Name'

Also, coming soon to the 'Exclusive Content' page: **Deleted Scenes** from the I AM MARGARET series!

If you have enjoyed the I AM MARGARET series, would you consider leaving a review on Amazon, Goodreads, or your favorite retailer? *Reviews really help people choose books, so a big thank you!*

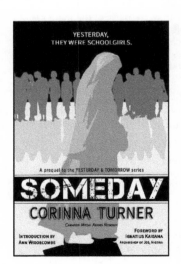

SOMEDAY

SNEAK PEEK 1—*GEMMA*

I open my mouth to reply to Annabel... break off, eyes widening at the sight of a uniformed—armed!—soldier rushing up the stairwell.

"Outside!" he yells, in some sort of thick, inner-city accent. "Hurry up, everyone out!"

"Is there actually a fire?" gasps Annabel, her ridiculously long hair tumbling all around her again as she almost drops her hair tie. "Not just mice chewing wires again..."

But Ruth frowns slightly as she looks at the soldier—yeah, he's not a fireman.

He sees our expressions. "There's been a bomb threat. *Out,* now! Where is everyone else?"

"There isn't anyone else," Annabel says over her shoulder, taking off down the stairs as though... she's just heard there might be a bomb in the building.

The soldier looks annoyed—yells after her, "Where are the younger ones?"

"Year seven are at an adventure training camp," I reply, but I start down the stairs as well. Bomb threats are usually hoaxes but I'm so not risking it. Not the way things are at the moment. "Year eight, IT camp; year nine, French exchange; year ten, Venice, English trip. It's just us and the sixth form."

The soldier swears loudly, and starts herding us back down the stairs, giving me a push to hurry me along.

"Hey!" I protest. "If I fall and break something and you have to carry me, it's going to take even longer, isn't it?"

Ruth shoots the man another looks and trots on down the stairs, guiding Yoko with her, like she's more scared of the soldier than of the bomb. And though I'd never admit it, I do kind of respect her opinion—at least on anything that doesn't concern the divine Sky Fairy.

The man's scruffier than any soldier I've ever seen—and since when do they dispatch armed men to evacuate civilians?

ALLELUIA

"Quit shoving, would you?" I snap at the man who's chivvying us towards the assembly point. "Think I wanna stay in there with a bomb, huh?"

"Hurry up," he says.

That's all he's said since he met us outside the sixth form block and I'm sick of it.

"Jesus loves you too," I tell him.

He smacks me across the head and I gasp in pain. Did this soldier seriously just hit me? Then I see the assembly point ahead and the words evaporate from my mind.

There's a row of trucks and a couple of horse vans—horseboxes, they call them over here—pulled up in the parking lot, and more soldiers are forcing girls into them at gunpoint. Everyone looks scared—a few girls are crying. *Lord, what is going on?*

"Show us some ID!" Miss Trott is yelling. She's the senior housemistress. "You are not taking these girls unless we see some ID! Where are the police? Where's bomb disposal?" She grabs a soldier's arm, "ID, *now!*"

The soldier un-shoulders his rifle and casually smashes the butt into Miss Trott's face. She crumples to the ground in a horrible, boneless way. I jerk in a shocked breath—then grab Jill and Karen. "*Run!*"

I shove them towards the wood and dive at the soldier who hit me—after a moment of confusion, I'm rewarded by the sound of Jill and Karen's running footsteps on the gravel path. The soldier shoves me away so hard I fall, tearing pajamas and knee. *Ow...* Blood oozes brightly across my black skin. But Jill and Karen have disappeared into the dark.

The soldier swings back to me—my heart freezes in my throat, everything freezes as he brings up the rifle and cocks it, hate filling his angry eyes...

SNEAK PEEK 2— *SAM*

We've spent hours trailing through any bit of woodland that can be accessed by road and we're scratched and footsore and frustrated. And hot. Of course we know ninety-nine percent of the searchers in the entire country won't find anything *and* we're being given the least likely areas, what with us being, like, the eighty-eighth line of defense or something—but I suppose we're all hoping—and dreading what we might find, at the same time.

Movement up ahead... my mind snaps back to the job at hand, heart lurching in hope-fear. It'll be nothing... it'd better be nothing, we're all unarmed... Take more than this for them to issue live ammo to university students.

The biggest excitement of the morning approaches... in the form of a teenage boy riding bareback—and barefooted—on a black and white pony. He rides right on up to our fatigue-clad selves in a way that makes me pretty sure he's heard nothing about the terrorists.

I can't help asking, "Why aren't you in school?"

"I don't go to school. I'm home-schooled. Or..." He grins. "Caravan-schooled."

"Oh, you're a gyp... traveler, right?"

"Half. My dad's a hippie. Traveler-wannabee, as my mum would say."

"Right. Well... Have you seen any horseboxes or vans back there in the woods?"

He gives me a funny look. "You're soldiers, right? Why are you looking for vans?"

"Yes, territorial army, strictly speaking—but we're just university officer cadets. We're looking for the two hundred and seventy-six schoolgirls who were kidnapped this morning. Or rather, the vehicles they were taken in, almost certainly abandoned, by now."

The boy greets this with a nod. "So this is like a role-play, or something, right? That you're doing for training? Is it okay for me to tell you where they are, then, or are you supposed to find them yourselves?"

"No, they've really been taken. By Islamist fanatics... *Wait*, are you saying you've *seen* some vans back there?"

"Yeah," he says slowly, eyes very wide. Then he shakes his head as though to banish his shock and turns the pony, puts it to a canter, calling over his shoulder, "This way..."

"Wait!" I yell. "You need to wait for us. Those men are dangerous."

He pulls the pony to a halt and looks us up and down. "And what are you going to do, spit at them?"

I try not to grit my teeth too hard. "We can at least make a cautious approach," I tell him, then call to the others, "Okay, stay in your line but we're following the pony. Double-time."

When the boy finally slips from the pony's back and throws his reins over a bush, we catch him up. "This way," he whispers, and glides off silently through the trees.

We follow, sounding like a herd of blundering elephants in comparison. But we soon come over a slight rise and there below us is a clearing...

My heart begins to pound. Three vehicles. Two white vans and a blue horsebox... God help us, it's an exact match! I hesitate, torn. We're under strict orders to call for armed backup if we find anything, but... I try the radio again. Nothing. No signal on my phone either. What have we got to report, anyway? There doesn't seem to be anyone here. It may be nothing to do with the kidnapping.

"Wrexham, come with me," I say softly. "We'll circle the clearing and see what we can see. Everyone else, stay here. Tanner, you're in charge. If someone shoots us, bug out and phone for help as soon as you can get a signal."

I pick up a sturdy branch and move down the slope towards the clearing. A stick's better than nothing, right? Henry Wrexham follows. The gypsy-boy has slipped all the way to the edge of the clearing and is peering from behind a bush. I'd better try and get him to stay back.

But as I move down towards him, I find that I can see the backs of the vehicles, and they're all open, the roll backs up on the vans and the ramp down on the horsebox. A prickle of unease runs up my spine. Okay, so it's really hot today, but it could just as easily be pouring rain. Why would someone leave their vehicles open like that?

The boy glances at me when I stop beside him. "Someone brought two really big vehicles up into this clearing sometime this morning," he tells me softly, pointing. "You can see the tire marks. Looks like semi-trucks. Totally unsuitable for that track."

Another cold prickle.

"Change of plan, Henry," I say. "We'll..."

But then a thin cry comes from the horsebox: *"Help..."*